CHANDLER'S DESTINY

my friend Dale Deslant

A.C. BASHAM

C-Boy

6/8/08

Llumina Press

© 2005 A. C. Basham

All rights reserved. No part of this publication may be reproduced or transmitted in any form or by any means electronic or mechanical, including photocopy, recording, or any information storage and retrieval system, without permission in writing from both the copyright owner and the publisher.

Requests for permission to make copies of any part of this work should be mailed to Permissions Department, Llumina Press, PO Box 772246, Coral Springs, FL 33077-2246

ISBN: 1-59526-002-1

Printed in the United States of America by Llumina Press

Library of Congress Control Number: 2005925541

DEDICATION

I am dedicating this book to my late wife,
Blusie Basham, and Barbara Talley.

Foreword

I was born in a sawmill town. A left-handed, redheaded, freckled boy from a set of twins, born on the same day and in the same year as Shirley Temple, which is my only claim to fame. We spent our carefree days in the woods and swamps around our home, hunting with guns and dogs, so we could help put food on the table. This was in the early Thirties and Forties and we were very poor. I began writing these stories so I could send them to my sisters because they hadn't heard many of them before. I have five sisters, strung out over almost thirty years in their different ages.

As I learned to write on the computer, communicating over the internet made it much easier for me to share my stories. Now my other

kin and my friends would like to hear my stories too, so with a little encouragement, I am pleased to be able to share them. I have always been an avid reader and have thought about being a writer, just like most readers do. I am a notoriously bad speller and typist and use country boy slang I call "red neck ebonics." Now these stories may not be PC but that's the way I talk. The sisters like the way I write and they can decipher it most of the time. I may put them in a book and then they'll have some rewriting and editing.

The second part to my stories tells about a place in a four state area called Ark.LA.Tex and talk about the fifty years I spent on and around oilfields. I worked side by side with two buddies, Chester Chandler and John Anderson, so I collaborated with them when it came time to tell this story.

The last part to my stories takes place right here in Toledo Bend and talks about my retired buddies; Bill Jug Donley and his little dog Louie (dubbed the "King of Mean") and Joe Henry Bryant, a fellow that was raised on peas. Not least One Half, Nancy, who encouraged me, and my sweet wife. She keeps us Old Boys straight.

Sunday, February 3, 2002. I use the penname C-Boy to sign my letters. My real name is A. C. "Red" Basham.

Chapter 1

Red Chandler was frantically throwing clothes and what few possessions he had in a small canvas bag. He was in a hurry to leave this place called New Orleans, where he had only landed six months before. He slipped out the back door of Rue 14, one block off Bourbon Street, and made his way to a pasture where he had been boarding his horse, Rusty. He saddled up, tied down his pack and was soon riding north, keeping a close watch on his back trail. He didn't want to push Rusty too hard, but he figured his pursuers would follow him until dark anyways.

The moon was out so he kept riding. He was following the old river road or "military road" as some called it. The country was mostly cotton farming with great plantations sitting back off the road a ways, shimmering majestically and ghostly through the large Evangeline oaks that guarded their entrances. Close to the road were sharecropper houses, most times built shotgun style. They all had a bunch of kids and a couple of big yard dogs that came out and raised a ruckus at his passing. The trick was to keep straight ahead. They knew not to bite a rider, but just to let the world know of your passing. Anyways, when one did get in range, Rusty would kick him a whack. After putting you a quarter of a mile on past their house they went on back home, prancing stiff-legged, their job well done.

About midnight he found a small clearing where Rusty could graze. He dug out a couple of biscuits from his pack. This would be a cold camp, as he didn't want a fire to be seen and by early dawn he would be up and on the road again. As he lay there on that ground listening to the night sounds, with his head using his saddle blanket for a pillow, he started reflecting back on how all this was happening to him now. It was the first time in his life that he was running, but it wouldn't be the last, not by a long shot. The smell of Rusty was strong on that saddle blanket, but that was good. He and Rusty had been together through hard times all their lives.

Chapter 2

He had come out of the Cane Breaks region of central Louisiana. His daddy was a lumberman and they always lived close to the swamps where he helped cut the big bald cypresses, which were used to build the great plantation homes mostly. It was called the *eternal wood*, as it wouldn't rot and termites left it alone. It was said that these tall majestic trees draped in Spanish moss were young saplings when Christ was on earth. In the clearing, after the trees were cut and sunlight could hit the ground, the switch cane grew up in almost impenetrable profusion; hence they were called Cane Breakers. They supplemented their living by hunting, trapping and fishing out of the big bayou. It was really a highway to the big river that had steamboats to where the lumber was shipped as needed.

Red was the youngest of several brothers and sisters. Kids came up doing chores at an early age. The girls helped mama with washing and tending to the baby; the boys took care of the big work mules, cut the firewood and hunted or fished for meat to put on the table. They had this saying; if they couldn't eat it they could sell the hide or sometimes both, such as a raccoon.

There weren't any fat kids in the Chandler family. They were of Scotch-Irish descent, out of the lower pinewoods of central Louisiana. They tended to be tall and rawboned till later in life and then they'd fill out. They ate a lot of fat in their diet; fresh pork was a staple and Mama fried a lot of food with rendered out pure lard, but they kept it worked off or run off, as a trip to anywhere was several miles away.

Red started helping in the lumbering. He was to trim the big trees after they fell and help cut them to length. He wasn't allowed to fell the timber yet, as this was very dangerous work. They usually had to cut notches in those big hollow butts, about twenty feet off the ground and stick in boards to stand on because they were too big at ground level for their saws to reach through. This made for very dangerous work because as the tree started to fall it didn't leave anywhere for the lumberjacks to run and the fatality rate was high. This is just what happened to Red's daddy one day.

Red's older brother had carved out a hill farm up close to Alexandria, Louisiana and carried their mama and sisters back to live with him. Red was nineteen at the time, considered a man in those days, but still very green about the facts of life. Hill farming wasn't for him and besides, there was a stirring in him that wanted to see a lot more of life. So he and his trusted pony Rusty, rode south and finally wound up in New Orleans.

Oh, the wondrous sights and sounds were breathtaking. This was much more than he had ever believed. The first thing to do was to find a place to live and then, surely with all the comings and goings, a job wouldn't be hard to find. He was informed that a Miz Cher Pluisant sometimes took in boarders at Rue 14 Street, not one block off Bourbon Street, in the heart of town.

Red soon found the house and knocked on the door. The door was opened by a Quadroon Creole woman that asked Red, "What you want, white boy?"

Red was taken aback by her savage beauty. The dark eyes, the big head of flowing hair that tended to run from waves to kinky, giving her a wild but sexy look that turned heads wherever she went. She always wore clothes that showed off her voluptuous body. Miz Pluisant was known to be independent. She wasn't married but had money and sent suitors scuttling with her stern stare. It was even said that she practiced voodoo.

She asked again, "What you want, boy?" She usually stared most men down, but standing before her was a six foot two, dark auburn haired, strapping of a young man.

Red didn't blink and said, "Pardon me madam, I was taken aback by your beauty. I was informed that you took in boarders from time to time."

He saw her face take on a slight smile and she said, "Come this way."

He would find out later how she got her money, but for now Cher had found just what she was looking for in a man, if she could mold him to her liking, and she was quite sure she could.

Chapter 3

Cher led him down a hallway bordered by a parlor and a library to a back bedroom of modest size. Everything he saw was upper class. He wondered how many borders she had and soon found that he was the only one. She then led him out to the kitchen were he met the Negro housekeeper, a plump, quick to be friends, woman.

Miz Pluisant says, "Pearl, fix the gentleman some ham and eggs, he looks hungry."

Cher watched Red eat and could see that she had a lot of molding to do with this giant of a man. A few months of Pearl's gumbos and fried chicken would fill him out and with a lot of her polishing, he would be the envy of the town and she would be on his arm. He hadn't been there an hour and he was in her debt already. Cher waved off the customary pay-up-front rent and told him to save his money while finding a job.

What Cher didn't tell him was she didn't want him working. She didn't want this handsome young man mingling with the common classes and getting captured by a saucy waitress, in some downtown bistro, that was in heat. You see she got her money as a kept woman of a white, middle age banker, from the largest bank in town and like most all kept women; it was a lonely life. She didn't love this man but did love the money, fine clothes and jewelry he gave her. Her passion was so great that every couple of weeks, when he came around, she threw herself at him so aggressively that his ego was built up to great heights. The banker was in love and very jealous, as most sugar daddies are.

The great challenge would be balancing her sugar daddy and her sugar man. Whee, what an adventure she was starting on; life was worth living again. The sugar daddy would never divorce his wife, as it would hurt him too much financially. Besides, a white banker would never marry a Creole in any case. She needed this young man to fill the great passion she had boiling within her. Yes, this shy but bold man would fit the bill. She needed an escort to the better restaurants, a protector. A lone woman, even a strong one that was known to carry a gun in her purse, was fair game to a drunk.

She had seen the sparkle in his eyes as he glanced at all her books in the library. She would find the depth of his intellectual curiosity real quick, educate him and tutor him for business. She would make him love her. She was sure he would never leave her bed and once he was successful, then he would marry her.

She would hold him at arms length for a while, until he wouldn't be held off any longer. Tomorrow she would buy him some dress clothes. His mornings would be spent in the parlor, reading and studying etiquette. The evenings would include strolls about town, getting first hand knowledge of the many cultures and how they mixed to coexist: some good and some bad, especially the gambling dens with their pimps and pickpockets. New Orleans didn't get its nickname, *The Big Easy*, for nothing and a lot of newcomers got lost in its world of humanity before they were aware of trouble.

Chapter 4

A week had went by and Miz Cher hadn't let him stop long enough to look for a job. She seemed to draw closer to him and him to her as each day passed. He found himself thinking of her as he went to sleep at night and could hardly wait for morning and her, waiting in the tropical garden patio out back. Pearl brought them their New Orleans coffee, half coffee and half hot cream, along with the special doughnuts that came from the cafe on Royal Street. They took carriage rides to the waterfront, ate in the waterfront cafes and rubbed shoulders with ship's captains from all over the world. There were Hindus in turbans and rough looking Turks with daggers in their belt. These were places Cher had not dared go alone before, as women were kidnapped and sold to Arabs for harems in far away lands. Most men were armed and she soon saw that Red could handle a gun. She guessed that his easygoing, laughable manner could change in a flash. She guessed right about that. He was no wimp. The trick was to keep him from appearing to be a gigolo, but instead just training for a job in the business.

Her boiling point for Red was getting close and besides, she wanted him in her total grasp before her sugar daddy's next visit and he was due any day now. If she satisfied Red's passion and then he found out she was a kept woman, he would be hooked and not leave her, if her next guess was right.

The next morning he was late for coffee. When he did show up, she could tell by the way he was looking at her that he was hers: lock, stock and barrel. She was right again. Things were going faster than planned. When her banker showed up that evening, she had sent Red out to buy himself another suit since she knew there was no sanger of him straying now, but her passion for Red was distracting. She made the mistake of just going through the motions; the banker wasn't pleased and left grumpy.

Chapter 5

A couple of months had gone by since Red had taken up residence with Miz Cher Pluisant and what a whirlwind life it had turned out to be. He had been tutored in living the good life and had eaten fabulous cuisines at the famous restaurants he thought were only in fairytales. He had rubbed shoulders with the near famous and thugs of the world. He had been tested by bigoted classes of old money, as well as the jealous lower class, for taking one of their fairest. He had poured over books, gaining knowledge about the many flags that flew over New Orleans. One thing that stuck in his mind was the unexplored West. The country of great stretches of prairie, mountains and finally an ocean so big that it took two years to cross and then return. It had many exotic things, like big fruit that had milk inside and was sweeter than cow's milk.

But all was not as good as it seemed. One evening as he and Cher were out strolling, she squeezed his arm and pointed out three known thugs that had been following them for some time. She was visibly frightened and warned him to be on constant guard. These three were backstabbers and as long as you had them in front of you, so to speak, they wouldn't make a move. It was common knowledge that there were no secrets in New Orleans, if you paid the price. Her sugar daddy had become more suspicious of her indifference, but that's the way women are when they fall for another man. He was surely on to them by now and with his money he could cause a lot of trouble. She had tried to convince him that Red was just a common boarder, escort and protector while she waited for his visits but his snitches told him otherwise.

Banking was in a slow cycle. His wife was off to Paris to shop and spend a lot of money. He was still paying Cher her monthly fees; he dare not stop and risk being told to stay away, as she was his whole world. He had even asked for weekly visit, for double the money and gifts, but was rejected. He was enraged even more and swore to get revenge.

Red had been meeting a lot of business people and one merchant had asked him to come in as half owner of a new steamboat that was being built. His up front money would be small. The steamboat would haul their merchandise and be assured a profit. He felt, for the first time that he was on his way as a businessman, and soon Cher could be his sole responsibility. He really never liked their relationship and her being with another man, but with her passion and love, he felt assured. The situation with the banker was just Cher doing her duty. Besides, look what fortune had befallen him for being understanding. He was in love and Miz Cher could tell him to leave as easy as the banker.

The first sign of real trouble was a note left on his pillow, warning him to leave or he would be very sorry. It was startling to say the least. They had to have let themselves in the house while he and Cher were out for the evening or could it be that Pearl had been bribed to place it there? Surely not, she had been a faithful servant of Miz Cher's for years.

He showed the note to Cher and she was shaken.

She said, "We must be very careful; he is very rich and powerful. He can have you killed and make it look like it happened in a robbery."

Cher thought, 'This isn't going as planned.' She hadn't planned on falling for Red. She could just tell him it was over. She thought she could control the banker easily enough by threatening to scandalize him, but most of all by withholding her favors. She hadn't figured on his blind jealousy.

The banker started sending threatening notes to Cher almost daily; threatening harm to Red and asking for her favors several times a week. Hell, his visits twice a month were about all the banker could handle but jealousy has no limits. She would have to put him off somehow.

She quickly planned a trip to Lafayette, Louisiana, hoping to let him cool off and come to some reasonable discourse.

They had ordered the carriage to show that evening. Red had made a fast trip to make sure that Rusty, his pony, would be taken care of in his absence. They would go by ship to Morgan City and then by carriage on to Lafayette. Red had never been aboard a schooner and was thrilled to be undertaking such a trip.

As he returned to Rue 14, the banker was dashing out of the house. He had a crazy look on his face and blood on his hands. Red's heart sank and his worst fear was about to materialize.

He grabbed the banker in an iron grasp and asked, "What have you done?"

The banker was shouting wildly, "If I can't have her no one will!"

Red dragged him back inside and there in the parlor laid Cher with a dagger in her back. Red's grief was overwhelming and before he could think, he pulled his pistol and shot the banker in the ear.

The world was spinning. His love was gone and he had just killed one of the most famous men in New Orleans. Pearl had run out of the house in hysterics. She had seen both killings. Red knew his time here was short. Funny how this newfound knowledge made life mean much more to him now. He quickly started packing and ran to round up Rusty.

Chapter 6

Red had found a good campground on the banks of Bayou Sara, about a half-mile out of town. He would live there in a tent and stay out of the mainstream of town. He really wanted to be alone to lick his wounds anyway. He hung his sporting suite up that night, to shake out most of the wrinkles, bathed in the bayou and shaved. He then presented himself at the Taggert sugar mill as Jim Sparks from up Alexandria way.

Zeb Taggert took an instant liking to this big redhead. He was a redneck like himself, and gave him the job of overseeing the timbering crews. His job was to clear the new land and cut the bottomland hardwoods into cordwood for the big hungry boilers at the big new mill. He had a mixed crew of blacks and Cajuns. They would be busy keeping those boilers fed, as this was an around the clock operation once it kicked off. He would ride Rusty to the mill and be there at daylight to make sure all the crews were ready. He would use Rusty as his overseer's mount and get an extra dollar a day for that. It would be easy on Rusty and he would always be close if he had to make a quick getaway.

Zeb Taggert was a power hungry man that knew farming best. He was a driver of people, but it was said that he drove himself even harder. He had worn out several hill farms and one woman up in Meridian, Mississippi. After his wife died, from being used up mostly, and the yield on the land shrinking every year: Zeb was ready to move on. He thought, 'Why farm that poor sandy clay land when there was deep delta soil to be had for cheap in inland Louisiana once you got away from the main rivers?'

Zeb Taggert was a user. He wore his wife out using her like a brood cow. She was almost always with child. She had hardly weaned one until she was fresh again. The first four children were boys, to Zeb's delight. He took them to the fields early. The next three were girls and they also went to the fields, except for one, who was left to help Zeb's wife. Her work started way before daylight; a big breakfast had to be on the table by first light, then the milking. The washing, mending and canning left her no time for rest. She was stooped over at forty years old, from bearing all those children, and she could count three that died early. One at childbirth, one at six years old and the other at seven. That had taken a heavy toll on her heart as well as her body. Zeb did see that only the boys had an education. He hired a live-in schoolmarm and it was rumored that she did more than teach school for Zeb. This may have broken Miz Taggert even more, but the cause of her death was just mostly she was wore slap out.

Zeb found what he was looking for in Bunkie, Louisiana. The land just north of town was hill country and populated with mostly transplanted Georgia crackers and he knew them well. The land south was rich delta and cheap as delta land goes. It was populated by the Catholic Cajuns that he would have to get to know quickly. He set himself up in the best boardinghouse and deposited his money in the 'old money' family bank in town and it wasn't long before the 'old money' was calling on him. There was new money in town and they were after Zeb's money, only they didn't know that this wily farmer was after theirs too. Their second and third generations had grown soft on their inherited money and Zeb would be the plucker in the end.

As Zeb made the rounds of the social circle, he was soon introduced to an upper class Cajun widow, about his own age. She had lost her husband to malaria just two years before and to sweeten the deal, she owned a five-hundred acre delta farm that was about to be foreclosed on by the good old boys at the First National bank, for only a pittance of its total worth.

Chapter 7

Zeb had found his starting place and if he could pull it off, he would have a leg up and for a pittance at that. He would woo the widow, marry her, pay off the mortgage and suck that plum right out of the 'old money's' greedy hands. There were acres of government land adjoining it at a good price.

Zeb married Miz Marie Cheramie, but this strong willed woman was his match. She was from landed gentry and a long line of Cheramie's. She would use this hard driving Zeb Taggert for her means also. She wasn't about to be his brood cow or take a backseat to this redneck farmer. They did have one daughter the first year and then Marie shut the childbearing off. She had him tied to any and all lands they might own, through this child, and that was it. This daughter was special from birth. A blond with green eyes and with the most flawless olive skin you've ever seen. She was the apple of Zeb's eye. He absolutely doted on her. He took her with him everywhere. She was the prettiest tomboy you ever did see. She was eighteen now and a head turning beauty, so Zeb guarded her like a hawk. No wimpy peckerwood or backwoods Cajun was going to have his beautiful daughter.

Zeb had only let his sons run with the most desirable debutantes. He had them married into the biggest banking family, the two biggest mercantile families in town and a family that owned the small packer steamboats that carried their produce to the big river. He could squeeze the adjoining farmers three ways: cut off their money, their supplies and their transportation. Yes sir, they had to come to old Zeb Taggert on just about anything they did. He was at the pinnacle of his power. He had also just built the biggest and most modern sugar mill in the South. Now he could control the sugar industry for miles around as well.

He was hoping to give his beautiful daughter a position managing his affairs. She would be so involved with it that men wouldn't interest her, but there is where he guessed wrong. She was a boiling bundle of raging hormones and just waiting for the right man and time to explore them together. Hell, with her bloodlines, what did he expect? He was as blind as most doting fathers are.

Chapter 8

Red had stopped in town that day, at the cafe on Main Street. He was ready for a good Cajun meal and maybe listening for any gossip that may be floating around on a wanted poster. He had made the near fatal mistake of not keeping his back to the door. As he was eating, he got this strange feeling that he was being watched. Have you seen a wild animal get nervous and look right at you even though you are completely hidden? He had that feeling and the hairs on his neck pricked up. He slid his hand under his jacket and grasped his Colt, and then he turned and was ready to have it out. He had made up his mind that he would never rot in a prison.

But low and behold, there standing across the room, was Leslie Taggert and she was staring at him. Most men wilted under that look, but Red didn't blink. He was dumbfounded and a chill ran over him. Here was another beautiful woman that had singled him out. He wondered why she was staring at him. He gave her a slight smile and she smiled back. She turned, walked out, mounted her thoroughbred jumper and was gone. Or was she? As he went past where she had been standing, there was the smell of an exotic perfume lingering in the air. He needed this like he needed a hole in his head, but he was sure he would see more of her whether he wanted to or not.

Leslie had found the man she wanted to explore those feeling with, but she was sure her daddy would never let her know any man that wasn't of his choosing. He would have to be rich and near famous but Leslie knew that she would never approve of any man that her daddy picked. She would be damned if she was going to wait under those circumstances. She was ready to know a man and this one fit the bill just fine. She had seen Red at work at the mill, knew he lived by himself on the banks of Bayou Sara and she knew just how she was going to arrange their first meeting.

Leslie Taggert could enjoy one thing that her father didn't chaperone her at and that was riding her fine jumper on the loop around the backside of the main house on the plantation. This day, she had the cook make her a picnic basket of fried chicken and a bottle of wine. As soon as she was out of sight of the big house, she turned her horse toward the east fence, gave him the signal and she was over the fence in a flash. She would be on the banks of Bayou Sara, about a half-mile out of town, in a few minutes.

Red was tidying up camp when Rusty let him know that they would soon be having company. He was almost sure who it was, but laid his gun within quick reach, just as a precaution.

Leslie rode right into camp and said, "Hello Red. "I brought you some supper; may I join you?"

She was dismounting at the same time and was wearing a gaucho riding outfit that even had the matching hat. She was gorgeous and that perfume. That perfume would stir a fire-and-brimstone Baptist preacher to life. As he took her basket, their hands touched and she was so warm. She felt like she could have a fever. Or was it him?

He said, "Thank you Miz Leslie."

She corrected him and said, "Just call me Leslie."

She came over and sat down beside him, with her leg touching the side of his leg. He was having trouble eating that fried chicken and he loved fried chicken. It wasn't long before the wine Leslie brought had the desired effect. Leslie had kept his glass a lot fuller than hers. He needed his, she didn't. As he finished a drumstick and turned to thank her, she kissed him full on the mouth. They made love there on the banks of Bayou Sara. She soon jumped up and mounted her horse, laughing at his bewilderment. She sank her spurs in her horse and was soon back on her daddy's land.

Chapter 9

Hardly a day passed that Leslie didn't ride by. Lots of days she would be there ahead of Red. She nearly always brought his supper: some very tasty dishes and good wines. This was living like a king, only in a tent by a slow moving bayou. She usually demanded that he make love to her immediately, or she just came to him in a rush and he had no choice. She liked to smell his sweat from the workday. They would usually swim and bathe in the nude, in the bayou. He would have the meal and wine she brought and Leslie would want to make love again before her quick departure. He was sure that she cared for him, but he felt kept again. He dare not lose his heart to her, as the milling of the sugar season was about over and he would be moving on. Still, in the back of his mind there hung this foreboding feeling of tragedy. He almost looked forward to the end of the season so he could draw his money and be gone.

He saw Zeb Taggert from time to time and always got a firm handshake and a 'good job' or 'well done' for his work. Sometimes Leslie would be at her father's side. She acted indifferent, like he wasn't there. He kind of had that feeling that the Mulatto's had. They would lay with you at night, but wouldn't speak to you on the street, in the daytime. They called it, 'How to recognize a Southern gentleman' in mockery, of course.

He felt that Zeb would want him to stay on as a sharecropper at the end of the season, but Red had seen how the sharecropper's books were kept. There were always two sets of them. One set of how a man actually did, which he never saw and one set that showed he had lost money, which he did see at the end of the year. He was furnished supplies out of the company mercantile store at high prices and they always showed that if he made 6 or 10 bales of cotton, he lacked half a bale of coming clear on the books. This kept him in debt. It was slavery, just under another name.

Bosses demanded that your whole family work the fields when needed and they owned you: lock, stock and barrel. Leslie had stayed away for a couple of days, but he had seen her moving around the big house on passing. Never-the-less, she was a shadow creeping through his thoughts. He packed his traveling bag for a quick getaway in any case, wore his gun at all times and was never very far from Rusty. After three days of being away, Leslie rode in one evening and Red could see the worry in her face. She just wanted to be held and petted a while. She gave out a few soft moans and finally told him that she was having morning sickness and would be showing in a couple more weeks. Her personal mammy had suspected Leslie's condition and tried to explain what was happening to her.

The mammy would hold her, cry and proclaim, "Oh, Lordy! What's Masa Zeb gonna do when he hears 'bout dis? Oh, Lordy, Lordy. Dare's gonna be a killin foe sho."

Red knew that when Zeb found out there would likely be a killing all right. He wanted to ride out of there while he could get a whole days head start. Then he would be sure that they didn't have any horses that could match Rusty's pace and they could wear them out in a week. But Red desperately needed the money he had coming. He had been foolish and not taken it each week like most. He would have to send some to his mother. Hell, he figured he had seen her for the last time over a year ago. He couldn't take the chance of leading a mad posse to his brother's farm and dragging him and his other kin in on this. That just wouldn't be right.

Leslie's mother now knew. She saw all the signs. Time was fast running out when they would have to tell Zeb and suffer his wrath. They knew that there would be suffering. Zeb would be fit to be tied at this news.

Chapter 10

When he went by the big house that morning, on the way to the mill, there were several carriages in the front. The sons had been called in and he could hear loud talk and cursing. Zeb was so devastated that he had turned on his daughter, cursing her and threatening to disown her. Zeb was demanding to know who the father was. Red quickly made his way on to the mill to ask for his pay. He knew asking three days early would be a dead give away. Damn almighty! Four months work down the river that he desperately needed. He would take the men out, slip back to his tent, get his traveling pack and be gone with great haste.

One of the sons finally found a fieldhand that knew something supposedly; a slacker. He had been hiding in the woods where Leslie jumped the fence each time she went to see Red. She had a well-worn trail, straight to his tent, on the bank of Bayou Sara. The four brothers mounted up. All were well armed and on their best horses.

Old Zeb ordered, "Find this man and bring him to me!"

Leslie saw them leaving. She quickly dressed up like a man, slipped out and mounted up. She took the back way out of the barn and once out of sight, spurred her horse into a dead run. She had to warn Red before they could capture him. Her daddy would torture him and then kill him. That day, she saw what a user her daddy really was. When she was no longer the great showpiece for him, he turned on her savagely and cast her out. He really loved no one but himself and power. She would go with Red.

Leslie took the longer route, but they were tracking through the woods. She felt she could beat them there, she just hoped she didn't kill her fine horse in the process.

She came riding into camp, her horse in a full lather and shouted, "Hurry! They will be here any minute and we must go!"

Red only took the things he had to have and quickly mounted up saying, "Follow me."

They took a woods path beside the bayou. The brothers rode up as they darted off. The chase was on. Leslie's horse was winded and her brothers were gaining on them. Red had to find a place for a stand-off. As she ran under a limb, Leslie lost her hat, clearly showing her long blond hair. Red headed for a cane break that he knew had a small opening in it and that only a fool would follow him in there. The brothers opened fire as Red and Leslie bent low in their saddles. They busted into the cane break opening and Leslie slid out of her saddle; she had caught a bullet in the back. The jealous bastards had murdered their own sister. Red knew they had seen her hair and had surely recognized it and her horse.

Red lost all reason. He walked out of the cane break as the brothers were circling and shooting into it, hoping to flush them out.

Red yelled, 'Over here!"

As they charged him, he killed two of them. The other two had enough and hightailed it out of there. He went back to Leslie and knelt by her side. He carried her out to the trail, laid her close to her brothers, mounted Rusty and set him in that running walk. He must go far away, since the blind rage of Zeb Taggert would never cease, but for Red, killing was getting easier.

Chapter 11

Red would head west to the new territory called Texas where the law wouldn't have any jurisdiction. He had killed some powerful men and their reach would be long. As for the banker in New Orleans, the upper class wailed and bemoaned his death for only a short time and then they went after his clients and money. They were like vultures, circling the kill and his widow would be lucky to be left a good living. It was mostly about money in that culture. They had chased the killer out of the country and besides; they figured the banker partly deserved what he got.

But those Taggerts would be very different. Zeb concocted a story that his daughter was raped by some ne'er-do-well cane breaker that had come to him broke; he had taken in, fed and given a good job. Then the black-hearted rascal had killed her and two of his sons. He was ashamed of his sons that had run, that didn't stay and finish the fight. At the same time, Zeb was well aware of the jealousy of his sons from his first marriage and after a lot of questions, the thought did occur to him that his own sons might have killed Leslie. Money and power had corrupted them as well. For a moment he thought that this big cane breaker would have been just what Leslie needed. She must have thought so. She had been riding to him and not the other way around. But Zeb's honor and prestige had been trampled and he must get that fellow, if it took the rest of his life. First he would call in his two son-in-laws and put his family back in the bank and the mercantile. He didn't trust many, but the Taggerts were closer than most and his daughters were dominant in their marriages too boot.

Next, he would write his brother in Laurel, Mississippi and ask for his help. He subsidized him on that wore out hill farm anyways. He just wanted to keep him from showing up in Bunkie and disgracing him. You see, his brother was illiterate, and people would snicker.

Zeb would ask his three nephews, a rowdy bunch and always in trouble, to follow Red's trail and to bring him back. He was sure that would be right down to their way of thinking they could serve their Uncle Zeb. At the same time, they would be getting away from the drudgery of that hill farm and be having some fun. He would outfit them well, give them fine horses from his stable, and turn them loose after getting them deputized in his parish. Course, that wouldn't be worth anything where they were going, but it would build their egos to get the job done. But who knew what would happen? If they found him in some territory with an incorporated town and a sheriff, they would get help. Lawmen had a strong code of honor to each other, whether right or wrong. The order would be plain and simple; get him dead or alive.

Chapter 12

Red pointed Rusty west and away from Bunkie. He figured Zeb Taggert would bury his dead, meanwhile spinning a dark story about Red to all that would listen. Red knew Zeb would swear revenge, on his own grave, if it took that long. First he'd want to save his family's pride and then send a message to anyone listening that to harm a Taggert would mean all the wrath that his money and power could summon.

Red entered the new territory of Texas about twenty miles east of Washington, Louisiana; an early trading town on Bayou Beaux. This was the last place small packet steamboats could come west out of the Mississippi. The hills joined the coastal plain here and an Indian trail went west, crossed the Sabine River and into San Antonio, a large Mexican village. Red was dodging all the settlements he could so as not to leave a trail that could be easily followed, but being a big man and a real redhead would make him stand out more than most.

It wasn't long until Red was in a region called the Big Thicket. It was easy to see how it got its name. It was a vast area above the Port of Houston and almost impenetrable. It was home to deer, bear, panther and the Red Wolf turkey, along with wild Longhorn cattle. He came to a settlement, astraddle the trail that you just couldn't go around, called Cut and Shoot. That put old Red on high alert. He had come far enough west that most men wore holstered guns openly and carried a chambered Winchester rifle. Red carried, but not to where his showed. They figured that anyone coming here was armed or a damn fool and wouldn't need a gun or anything else very long.

There were six families in this settlement, all big families, so it had a good population for its size. He got a friendly welcome. The most people were in two families: the Tallys and Donleys, who had married into each other's families. They were headed up by Bill Tally, a tough looking character, with a ready smile and handshake.

Redheads just seem to always be a friendly lot. They're what some called the 'salt of the earth' and besides a lone stranger was not a threat to these hard-bitten settlers, who were hunters and outlaws themselves. They figured a lone stranger that passed this way was on the run. They would quickly take his measure and if they liked him, they would ask him to stay awhile. If not they would abide by the code of the west: feed him, rest his horse and then send him on his way with a stern warning not to return. That was always enough.

Bill Tally told the women folk to rustle up some grub and sent a teenage boy off to feed and shelter Rusty. After they fed Red, and before he could leave the table, the whole big family had gathered around in silent anticipation of hearing news about anything. It wasn't considered good manners to ask questions, as a man's business was his own, unless he wanted you to know. That was another code of the west. Red had taken his real name of Red Chandler back, as the Taggerts would be looking for Jim Sparks. Maybe he shouldn't have but that was the first name that popped in his head. Jim was an old buddy from long ago that had gone Yankee. Yankee's weren't any good anyways and Jim could never come back and be accepted. The war had left very bitter feelings.

Red knew that right then he was being sized up to see if they asked him to stay or not. They were hungry for any kind of news and Red could blather on, as was his want, when it pleased him. Besides, there were a lot more good meals that these ladies could fix. You could live on trail food for only so long and then you had to have some boiled vegetables. So Red cut loose. He figured he could tell them about New Orleans. His main worry would forever be those Taggerts. If a couple came west looking for Red and he killed them, they would just send a couple more. The man of many glances would have to be vigilant as long as he was alive.

He gave them a little politics, but he knew the ladies wanted to here about the latest fashions, and the ladies were the one's who did the cooking. The trick was not to look interested in their women folk. You never made eye contact with them and only talked to the men and children. He did notice a rough around the edges, stout beauty, that was staring at him more that usual.

Bill said, "You kids have heard enough for now. Let Mr. Red rest for now."

Red said quickly that he would pay for his lodging and help do any chores that they might have that he could do.

Chapter 13

The next morning at breakfast, Red learned that the men folk were in to rounding up the wild Longhorn cattle that had become wild as deer and populated the whole South Texas gulf coast. They were brush poppers and offered Red a job helping them. It was wild, dangerous work that most didn't have a taste for. They told him that they would outfit him with a horse and chaps. Red really didn't have much of a choice if he wanted to stay and as long as they furnished the horses, he would give it a try. He dare not use Rusty, as this was crippling work and a horse was fast used up. He could make a little money, as they sold the cattle to a dealer for a dollar a head. After driving them to the port of Houston, they wound up in New Orleans and Mobile, Alabama. These were five-year-old cattle that had never seen a brand and were anybody's that could catch them.

The easiest way was to bay them with the specialized stock dogs that they raised. Red kind of knew how this went, as they did the same thing with the semi-wild hogs that ran loose in the swamps and waxed fat on the acorn mash. Only these were four times as big and had long horns that they sometimes killed a bear or panther with. These dogs are called Black Mouth Curs or Yellow Curs. They were a careful mixture of several breeds, hence the cur in their names. Once they got the mix just right, they guarded their lineage very closely. They always had puppies around, as a lot of dogs got killed or crippled.

They were big dogs, part hound: for a good nose and loud voice and part bulldog: for a broad head, strong jaws and the fierceness to catch when told to, along with the spotted or leopard spotted shepherd for herding instinct and faithfulness. A lot of them had agate blue eyes and were called 'glass eyed.' They trailed the wild cattle and bayed them. You rode in close, lassoed the steer, tied them to a tree, left them for a couple days, until they were simmered down and weakened from thirst and could be driven out to a corral. Some were tied to an old ox and he would bring them back.

Another way, and the hardest for sure, was when the brush was thin enough, all the riders would fan out and ride slowly abreast. Those horses could smell those steers and would slip along all a tremble, anticipating the chase. When you caught sight of a steer, the horse charged them and put you up alongside so you could rope it. The steer, being wild, broke for even heavier cover. You had to be stouthearted indeed, to hang in there while roaring through the brush and brambles. That night, as they had a pull or two on a corn liquor jug, there was great mimicking and hurrahing among some who laughed at being in their scary predicaments as the chase unfolded.

Red had never done much roping before this, but he was learning fast. The throws were short and quick or you were out of luck on that steer. The first charging rush almost always had to do the trick. Damn almighty, a fellow could get killed at this game.

Red lingered at the table by himself one evening, for too long. He was cleaning his Colt and the buxom wife of one of Bill's sons had been staring at him.

She came out of the kitchen with an extra piece of pie and placed it in front of him saying. "I thought you might want something extra sweet."

He was startled. Why just being caught alone with her would be enough for a skinning. Damn almighty, he couldn't stay in Cut and Shoot very much longer. If he got caught with this woman it would be a death sentence. If he spurned her, she might lie to get revenge. Either way, Red wouldn't like the outcome.

Chapter 14

Red fell in with a tough and fearless little fellow, by the name of William Donley, who was just called Jug for short. It seems that when Will was a young lad, some immigrants were coming through the settlement and the dogs spooked one of their wagons. The mules tried to run away and in the process, bounced that wagon around pretty good. Things were falling out of that wagon and one of them was a jug of rum. Well, Will grabbed up the jug and him and his buddies hid it in the brush. From that time on, he was called Jug Donley and he always had a taste for rum.

Jug and Red were just naturally drawn together. Jug was from South Carolina, had a past and was surely running from the law or something. Could be a family feud that had gone deadly. Jug's weakness was cat fishing. There was a good size stream a couple of miles from Cut and Shoot. Here they were called rivers or cricks, as these were mostly Irish and Scottish descendants. Jug was in hog heaven while setting out bank poles and trying for them big catfish.

They would cut stout poles, fifteen feet long, tie on heavy cord, a hook and bait them with a piece of rabbit or a crane meat they'd killed on the way there. They'd stick them poles in the sloping bank, deep enough to hold a big catfish, which were sometimes in the twenty pound range. This was usually done at night, as that's when the catfish bite best. There was usually several big lads that begged permission to accompany Jug on his and Red's trips. They were appointed to get the bait, prepare it and cut the poles. This was high adventure for them. Jug took over selecting the best holes or deep pools for the bank poles and their depth.

This was all done before dark. The poles were strung out over a quarter mile of creek bank. Wood was gathered to last the night, as it got very dark in those big woods, then the coffeepot was put on to boil.

They just used creek water and then dumped in a handful of that strong coffee with added chicory and set it aside. Jug would cut a green stick and place it in that coffeepot to settle the grounds to the bottom. You kind of strained it through your teeth anyways. Jug was a constant coffee drinker when it was available.

Fat pine torches were their only light. They scoured the woods and found old pine logs that had fallen, been cut down and had rotted, leaving only the rich skeleton in the middle. They called these 'pine lighters' and made torches out of them. A couple of torch bearers, one in front and usually Jug and one behind, carried a torch with their arms stretched over their heads, so as not to be blinded by the light as they tried to find the poles and not step on a Cottonmouth snake. The snakes came out at night, hunting bullfrogs.

When a pole was found all bent over and pulled under, Jug would grab that pole and if it was a big one, Red would grab his belt and help him back up that slippery bank. Jug would be hollering, "Hold the lights up," as sometimes it could be a gator. The poles were run about every hour and a half. In between, they gigged frogs or sat around the fire listening to tales of Jug and Reds exploits. Jug really liked to flower his up for the boys. Sometimes a panther would cry out and the night would go completely silent for a minute. All the creatures wanted to hide then. The boys would exchange nervous glances and the fire would be built up. Jug would tell a panther story to the boys and that bought them even closer to the fire.

Along about three o'clock in the morning, the boys would start nodding off, as the 'skeeters weren't so bad in the cool night air. If they really had a good catch, one of the boys went after a wagon. They would come in the next morning after daylight, all muddy and sooty from those pine torches, but triumphant as heroes. You see, those catfish were treasured for their good taste, being a break from their normal diet, and everyone shared in the big cook out.

The Cut and Shooters farmed enough to furnish themselves with fruit and vegetables, raised corn for bread and grain for their mules and horses, but they were mostly hunters and gathers. There was no cotton raised here nor stoop labor for these free-spirited folks. They did trap and another one of their great pastimes was varmint hunting for them wily old 'coons. Their hides sold well and they were also very tasty. These cur dogs were natural hunters. You had to break them from a pup to make them stock dogs, as they loved a 'coon fight.

'Coon hunting was another of Jug's passions. In fact, Jug's mother was a full blooded Cherokee Indian, so that's where he figured he got the natural instincts to find his way in the dark woods at night. If it was fair, he used the stars. If not, and you got too turned around, you found a creek. If you went into the woods south of the main trail, you just followed it up stream; you would eventually come back to that main east and west trail and to home. A few times they were so far off path that they just built a fire, spent the night and found their way out in the daylight.

A funny episode happened one night. The dogs had treed a 'coon up a big, tall, scaly-barked, hickory tree. The trick was to get the 'coon to look at your torch and shine his eyes, to locate him up that tree. If it was a small tree, they chopped it down and let the dogs have a good fight, as that made them eager hunters. But a tree as big as this, you shined his eyes and shot him out.

On this hunt Jug says, "I got him shined and he's a big one. Come shoot him Red, while I hold the torch."

If the 'coon turned away, Jug would mimic a mad 'coon and the 'coon would turn back for another look.

Well sir, Red let fly at that 'coon and Jug says, "You hit him and he's coming down."

The only thing was, when he plopped to the ground, this wasn't a 'coon, this was a black bear and he was mad as the devil. The dog and bear fight was on. These big part bulldog crosses would fight anything and it was a good thing too, as the young torch bearers took off. There were Jug and Red, with that bear fight raging all around them in the dark. [Author's note: This wasn't funny.] That bear growling and them dogs bellowing and yelping from getting clawed by that bear. It was hard to tell which way to back up, as the fight was in motion all around.

Red backed into Jug in the dark. Red's reaction was to swipe at the thing that brushed him with his gun butt and he gave old Jug a glancing blow. Jug let out a yell, that they later said, was heard a mile back in Cut and Shoot. That bear finally give up the ghost after that rifle shot, but not before a couple of their best dogs were mauled. Red and Jug had broken out in a sweat and it was a cool night. They got the torch bearers back, built a big fire and spent the rest of the night there. They needed help getting those crippled dogs and that bear back home.

Chapter 15

Red had been settled down here in Cut and Shoot for several months now and he felt fairly safe there. He knew if any strangers showed up, before they would be aware of him and he would just melt into the woods and stay in one of their shacks by the catch pens until they moved on. He had confided in Jug Donley and a few trusted more and Jug had spread the word to watch for anyone going by the name of Taggert. They would protect this big redhead that they had all grown to like so well. They took turns anyways, watching the penned up wild cattle, as they would be easy prey in the pens for a big panther.

Red had gotten caught up in this wild hunting and catching wild cattle, along with the hunting and fishing. He and Jug rode down to the Port of Houston every now and then. They blew off some steam, picked up coffee and flour, cartridges for the boys and trinkets for the girl children.

But things were developing in Bill Tally's house, where he boarded, that told him that the time was near when he would have to move on. To make things worse, his other best pard Leroy was the husband of that buxom, thirty year old woman that wanted to posses him. She had started primping before meals and would sit straight across from Red at that long narrow table. She would touch him on the foot or leg, under that table. He was just twenty years old now and it was hard for him to hide his feelings, which ran all from passion to being scared as the devil. He ate quickly and didn't linger after meals. He would hunt up Jug and have a smoke of that strong home grown tobacco. He latched his door at night now, as one night there was someone stirring in the hallway and his door was tried. Damn almighty, he never slept another wink that whole night through.

It would become obvious to the other women soon, if it wasn't already. You can't fool them on these things, they pick up on the slightest signals.

Red and Jug had become such good pards and since he didn't have a wife either, it was agreed that they would pull out together. Jug was antsy about staying in one place too long also. They had saved up enough money for supplies and a couple packhorses. They could travel leisurely and in comfort and see those far mountains that they had been told about. They would hunt the last of the buffalo and a strain of bear, bigger than you ever seen. First they would pass through San Antonio and see one of those fiestas and a couple of those dark eyed senoritas they had heard about, and try some tortillas and frijoles with lots of pepper.

It was agreed between them that they would announce a trip to the Port of Houston for supplies, take their two packhorses along, packed separately with their travel gear. Red would ride Rusty on their return. He would tell them that three strangers had landed off a ship from New Orleans and were asking about a Jim Sparks. They would say their goodbyes quickly and head west.

It was sad leaving. He and Jug had made lifelong friends here. They were Uncle Jug and Red to the boys and girls. The boys were holding back tears. They would miss those fishing and hunting trips and the camaraderie, but they had been taught well by Jug and could carry on by themselves. The girls just let go. Miz Tally was crying too. You made close friends when you lived this close. They swore to come back in a year or so, but knew in their hearts that the odds were against that ever happening. Betty Tally was nowhere to be seen. Red glanced toward the big house and saw her face against the window. He tipped his hat and quickly looked away; a love that could never be. He had only bit the bullet this time, he didn't have to use it.

Chapter 16

Red and Jug were soon out of the big timber country. It was fascinating to be able to see so far. A big open plantation was the most open land they had ever seen before. It surely wasn't nothing like the dark tall timber, where the wind moaned through the treetops a lot of the time. The wind blew here almost all of the time, but it was a lot dryer wind and it wasn't as bad, even though it was hotter than the humid gulf coast.

They were following the freight and immigrant road to San Antonio, Texas. They were riding through rolling hills with large outcroppings of sand and limestone. The valleys were well watered with springs, had good grass and a new kind of deer that was a lot bigger than the wood deer. Jug hollered out at the first one they saw, "Look at that reindeer!" They were antelope and along with wild goats and wild turkeys, they were everywhere and could be had with little effort. They only took what they needed. Jug Donley had those far seeing blue eyes and he could shoot the head off a turkey at seventy yards. It would be a very short time until Red saw just how good a shot old Jug really was.

They meet a couple freight wagons the very next day and were told to be on the look out for a group of ten to twelve banditos. The banditos had jumped the wagons in a shootout and one of their men was killed, but they had gotten two banditos. The only law from now on was Mr. Colt and Mr. Winchester, which were both in the same caliber and made it easier buying cartridges. The next day, they passed a new grave beside the road and became much more watchful.

They made the near fatal mistake of letting their guard down. The trail went by a limestone outcropping and dead ahead the ground was clear. The sun was shining right in their faces and the reflection off that white limestone was blinding. They pulled their hats down low and lowered their heads. The bandits had chosen their place and time well. They were too close to run before Rusty smelled them and gave them away.

They swooped down on them in a rush. There were ten in all and they had Red and Jug surrounded before they knew it. Jug turned his horse back toward the pack string. Red was already grasping the Colt under his vest. Jug's pistol was still in his holster, but he had loosened the tie strap and loosened it in its holster. These were an arrogant bunch of bastards. They figured that with ten of them surrounding Red and Jug that they had them intimidated and it was easy picking.

They were Indian and Mexican crossbreeds that owed no allegiance to anyone but their bulling leader and themselves. They were cold-blooded killers of everyone they robbed. Or they may take young women, if there were any, use them for several days in the most awful manner and then kill them too. They usually didn't bother the little native villages, just extracting tribute as lodging and food.

After a successful robbery, the bandits would take anything they could sell, push the stock back to San Antonio and sell it; no questions asked. Then they would drink and whore until they were broke and have to ride out again.

One of the weaseliest ones reached over with a stiletto to rip open one of the pack coverings. He never made it; Jug's hand was a blur. He killed him and one more in a flash. At the same time, Red killed the two facing him and made sure he shot the leader first. It happened so fast and the others were taken aback, to see their leader fall. They spurred their horses and with a wild yell and scattered four ways. A couple went across the open hillside. Jug dismounted, grabbed his Winchester, knelt down and waited until they were a couple hundred yards and winged both of them. Six shot, out of ten, wasn't bad. Damn almighty, he hoped he always had old Jug on his side in a gunfight.

The only thing of value, beside their horses, was a new Winchester rifle and two bandoliers of cartridges that they carried for the new forty-five, seventy-caliber rifle. They figured they had killed for that rifle. It might come in real handy one day, maybe on

a big grisly bear, after they reached the mountains they were headed for. They would sell the horses in town and no questions would be asked of them either. Their reputation would precede them. Two bad hombres were headed toward town. Red had five notches on his gun now; he was sure Jug had more than that, but wasn't about to ask him. Yep, killing them that needed killing wasn't so bad.

Chapter 17

San Antonio wasn't much of a town as towns go, but it was astir with intrigue. The country was really filling up after the war, but it was still a very wild and tough country. This was the jumping off place for the southwest desert.

They would stay only long enough to rest their horses and get supplies. They would go on west, strike the foothills of the Rocky Mountains and turn north. Those banditos had spread the word and they felt safer on the trail than in a town of this size. If the Taggerts showed up, they could find informants and help by the droves and at a small price. Life sold cheap hereabouts.

Red found out another thing or two about his little buddy. Jug had a knack for languages and was soon talking the native Tex-Mex Spanish lingo. Jug also loved those tortillas and frijoles. This was an improvement, as he believed Jug could live on plain strong coffee. So Red learned to do the trail cooking quickly, if they were to eat halfway decent meals. Jug did the hunting, with his sharp shooting; the game only had to pause and Jug could get supper. He also picked up enough Mesquite wood for the evening fire.

Cooking had its privileges. They used one iron skillet to make bread and cook stews in. They roasted the game right over the flames, so the only clean up was rinsing out the coffee cups. Jug said the cups added flavor to the coffee with the black stain left in. Red took a little sand to that skillet and the two tin plates, rinsed them and the dishes were done.

They set a leisurely pace and soon arrived at Fort Stockton. They fell in with a cow outfit that was getting a herd of Mexican cattle from Lathe, a fording place on the Rio Grande River, between Mexico and Texas. They were mostly stocker cows and bulls, with a few steers thrown in, for meat for the cowboys. They would also use some to placate the Indian tribes in the Oklahoma territory for safe passage.

The Indians were starving on their reservations and being shortchanged by the government. They were desperate and charged for passage and grazing rights.

They were the Lazy Bar Eight outfit and their brand was an eight laying on its side on a slash. They were taking these cattle to Cheyenne to stock a beautiful mountain valley. These cattle were real green and hadn't really been trail broke yet and they needed help. The ramrod seemed like a good sort and they threw in with them. They would go north for a while, then drop off for the big mountains; it would be a good deal for them both. They could surely use their help now and later they could get along with just their hands as the cattle got trail worn.

First they had to brand all the cattle; three thousand in all. What a job. They were given a work string of horses, about ten each. Turns out, they were green too. There was a rodeo every morning while riding out to the herd. The Eastern horses that Red and Jug were used to were a lot easier to break than these four-year-olds that had mostly run wild. Even the ones that had been broken just had to kick up from time to time.

You had to be vigilant all the time. They were crafty devils too. They would catch you too relaxed and buck you off in a flash. The regular cowboys got many a laugh out of Red and Jug, until they caught on. Red and Jug thought they were tough, but you rope and brand full grown cows all day long, then stand your turn at night guard and sleeping on that thin bedroll was like what heaven must be.

You only worked a horse a half a day and you used only one gait. You went from a lope to a full run all the time, except when you was riding night guard cause then it was slow and easy, round and round that herd. Some sang to them cows. Red could play a French harp and he played them cows every song he ever heard in his life. This kept the cows pacified and not listening to a lone coyote howl and want to spook.

The other cowboys liked to have night guard with Red, as you could hear that French harp for a long way out there on that open prairie.

Jug was thriving. They had a Mexican cook and his favorite dish was tortillas and frijoles. To boot, Jug could keep learning his Tex-Mex lingo. The branding was all done and it wasn't too soon to suit Jug and Red. They was wore to a frazzle. There was a few cattle in every herd that were always wanting to break away and were natural leaders. They were up and through grazing and ready to go, so you just headed them due north and started the others behind them. Cow punching wasn't so bad they thought, but they hadn't forded a river yet or seen a stampede.

They were jumped one night by some rustlers. They would ride into the herd, run off with a hundred or more, pushing them hard. They figured you wouldn't think it was worth the fight to get them back. But they hadn't figured on this ramrod. Dave Basham was a tough Irishman and by God, his boss sent him after three thousand cows and he was gonna get near that many or die trying. He asked for volunteers and Jug was the first and Red wasn't about to let his little buddy get into a fight without him. One more had said he would go. The boss told the rest to take the herd, go up to a nearby river, rest the herd on this side and wait for him. Red, Jug, and J.T. Anderson took up the outlaws trail. Red had saddled up Rusty for this nasty piece of work. He would see Red through if any horse could and he would alert them of strangers in plenty of time, so they wouldn't be surprised themselves.

The outlaws had pushed the cattle hard all the rest of the night and following day. They had watched their back trail and hadn't seen anything. They had run the cows into a box canyon and had even left their campfire glowing. The plan was to draw back. They figured the outlaws would be wore out and tired, along with the herd. They would wait until they were sound asleep, ride in slowly as close as they could get, and then charge in with guns a blazing. No quarter would be given, as there wasn't any doubt about it, they had the right bunch. They would ride over the whole camp not stopping; jump the cattle out of that canyon and head for the main herd.

They got pretty close before one of their horses gave them away and one of the outlaws sat up. Dave said, "Now," and they charged the camp, two on one side and two on the other, with guns a blazing. There were about six and they figured they got one apiece. Jug thinks he got two. They were back with the cattle in a flash and up and running. They let them run a ways but they were soon tired and slowed down. They turned them toward the main herd and drove them in late the next evening. The other cowboys took over and were very much relived to see their pards all in one piece. Red and Jug had risen several notches on their stick.

The cook fixed up a big supper of beans and steak. The three were relieved of night duty that night and they were soon asleep. Range justice had been done, another notch for Red and maybe two for Jug. Killing those that needed it was getting to be a regular job. Damn almighty!

Chapter 18

Young Bart Collins was the boss' nephew. He had begged all the previous winter to accompany his uncle Dave on this cattle drive. His mother and Mr. Dave had finally relented. He would go as a cook's helper and drive the supply wagon. He was seventeen and a stout boy, willing and eager for any task. You could tell his Uncle Dave was proud of him. It wasn't long until he was begging his uncle to let him be a full hand and ride herd with the other men. Mr. Dave gave in, cut him out his own string of mounts and started him riding drag. If he could take following three thousand head of cattle, smelling their droppings, choking on that dust, pulling his share of night guard, then and only then would he raise his pay to one dollar a day.

They were up on the Oklahoma line, fixing to cross into Kansas. It was getting close to the time for Red and Jug to go their way. That evening, away across the prairie in the northwest, a tall bank of blackish clouds had been building taller and taller. There was a change in the air; the cattle sensed it and they were nervous and balling more than usual. This looked like they were in for a rough night. They had had a pretty easy go of it all told. The horse Ramada was brought in and the cowboys came in as quick as they were relieved and got fresh mounts. All the hands would be out with the herd until this blew through.

About dark, a cool wind started blowing, so it wasn't far away now. The clouds had gotten darker, there were huge flashes of lightning seen and it would soon be on them. They had bunched the cattle in tight. Their lowing was constant and even though the cattle were tired, they refused to lie down. As the raging storm burst over and around them, the hail came down and it was big enough to smart. Then a huge crash of lightning came and the cattle were off. There was no holding them and they exploded in a dead run in an instant.

The leaders broke out in front of Bart and J.T. Anderson. Bart charged them to turn them and start them milling; like he had heard the older men talk about. Out of foolishness or trying to prove that he was a real hand, he charged too deep into the herd and was trapped. All his horse could do was run with them. J. T. had tried to cut him off, but was too late. He was soon lost from sight, never to be seen alive again. The only light at all in the dark night was when the lighting flashed about. You just had to trust your night horse to get you through.

It was over after a couple hours. They had finally gotten the cattle milling, but they were scattered all about. Each rider stayed where he was. He would bring in what cattle he could at daylight, give a report and hunt down stragglers all day. All reported in by late morning, all but young Bart. The boss man was frantic. He was dashing about, sending the men back out as soon as they got fresh mounts and a bite of grub. J. T. Anderson was beside himself, as he felt responsible for Bart.

They wore themselves out, searching all day. They began to fear the worst. Along in the evening, a cowboy was bringing in a bunch and as cattle got to a certain spot, they balled, split and went around it. He rode up to check the spot, knowing what he would find. It was even worse than what he expected. It looked like the whole herd had trampled Bart and there was hardly a thing left. The hand came on in, sidled up to Red and broke the bad news.

Red and Jug walked over to Mr. Dave and said, "Mr. Dave, we aren't trying to run your business, but Bart has been found. Would you let us bring him in for you?"

Dave knew it was bad and his grief was overwhelming. He agreed. They got a couple of Bart's blankets and were shown the spot. There was so little to pick up. They took one blanket, rolled up some prairie grass, added some dirt and then rolled that up in the other blanket. It was bad enough on Mr. Dave, they didn't want him to think there was nothing to bury. They brought him in a spare wagon. They had already dug a grave, on a high knoll beside another grave, so Bart wouldn't be alone. They put the rest of his bedroll under him and covered him up. The boss asked Red, as the most vocal one in the group, to say a word or two.

Red muttered, "Sure boss."

They took off their hats and bowed their heads. Red gave them these words.

"Oh Lord, take young Bart and give him a job with you, riding herd over all them angles you have. He is a damn good hand. Amen."

Mr. Dave and John Thomas turned away, but not before you could see where tears had washed the dust off their faces, leaving a clean streak. This was a tough moment, but it wouldn't hold a candle to when Mr. Dave had to tell Bart's mother.

It was a somber evening at supper. The cook had done his best to cook a good meal. The boss did a thing that's never, ever done in camp. He got out a jug and gave every hand a good pull from it. He then went back to bossing and reassigned night guards. They had a heard to get to Cheyenne. That night while on night guard, Red played the Cowboys Lament:

Oh bury me not on the lone prairie.
Where the coyotes howl
and the wind blows free.
Oh bury me not on the lone prairie.

Chapter 19

The herd was only a short ways out of Dodge City, when the boss called a couple days of rest, to get the men spirits up after their great loss. Half the boys would go in one day and the other half the next day. Red and Jug got first leave. The boss advanced them enough to have a good time on, but to not go slap wild and the cook went in for supplies. He was told to look up the sheriff and tell him he would pay any fines they may incur, but to just get his boys back to him in one piece. They still had a long way to go and had to beat the snow flying winter that comes early in the high country.

The first thing was to go by the barbershop, get a shave, a haircut and a bath. The Tumbleweed Saloon had it all. Ladies of the evening, gambling and about any kind of imported liquor you ever heard of, but the women wasn't gonna mess with any cowboy that hadn't had a bath in weeks. They were rough, but not that rough. Red and Jug burst through the doors, ordered a drink, Jug his beloved rum. He told the bartender to not make them very strong, but bring a lot of them. Red was sipping on a Jim Beam, a classic bourbon. The ladies swarmed them, since they knew they were coming and had prepared themselves. Jug was soon gone upstairs, but was just as soon back. It had been a long dry spell for him, in more ways than one. Now he could settle down to some serious drinking.

Red had a gal on each side. They were a four or a low five, on the scale of things, and Red was getting primed on that Beam. He was trying to make up his mind, which one was the best, when the back room door opened and out came a nine and one half. Yeah, buddy. She turned out to be the singer, Donna. She sashayed over to the piano and asked what everyone would like to hear. An old rebel yelled *Dixie*. She informed them that she sang better if they all had a drink. There was a rush to the bar. She handled her job well.

She had it all and while she was singing, she discovered Red standing in the middle of that bar. A look came over her face that Red had seen twice before. She was thinking, 'What a man. I will make him make love to me.' Red took a deep pull on that Beam. He wasn't gonna play dodge this day. After the song, she walked straight for Red, but on the way the house dandy and card shark tried to approach her, but she brushed him aside. It turned out that she was his girl and private stock. He was jealous as hell and he should be, but Red was lusting and didn't catch his mean look. Seems this guy was also a backstabber, but like all of his kind, Red knew as long as you had him in front of you, he wasn't gonna do any harm.

Donna told the other girls to get gone.

She sipped a drink with Red and whispered, "Let's go to my room."

The Beam was catching on and he said with a big grin, "Jug, I will see you in a little while, little buddy."

She had this room that opened on a balcony, with a glass door. They wasted no time and afterwards, while they were resting, she kissed him and said, "You made my day."

Red replied, "Pretty lady, you just made my year."

Red saw a man walk up to that glass door and he reached for his Colt. The bushwhacker raised his gun and fired, but like shooting through water, the glass made the angle distorted and he missed Red and killed Miz Donna. But Red wasn't shooting through the glass, that weasel had blown it out, and Red had a clear shot. Red pumped two in him. The first one pushed him back against the balcony and the other carried him over it, sprawling him in the street below. Red was dressed quickly, but Jug was already mounting the stairs.

Red said, "Little buddy, we gotta go," and they backed out of there.

They had to walk over the dandy lying in the street to get to their horses. They were not long leaving Dodge, but they really needn't worry. The dead man had a bad reputation and word had spread. The town was glad to be rid of him, but their great loss was Miz Donna. Damn almighty! Another notch, but this one needed killing too.

Chapter 20

Red and Jug rode back to the cow camp and they told Mr. Dave what had happened. They apologized and told him that they would be cutting out in the morning. It was time anyways and they didn't want to cause the outfit any trouble. They knew if a posse came after them, that all the cowboys would help them. They didn't have to worry. Red was a hero of sorts in town, and no one was happier than the Sheriff, to be rid of that cheating bully.

They had already arranged with the cook to get their trail supplies and they would have it deducted from their pay. Mr. Dave tried to talk them in to staying on. He didn't need them, but they had grown to really like little Jug and big Red. Mr. Dave said the land was for the taking and later on they could find them a broad valley and just claim it. He would give, or sell them a few head of cows at cost, to get them started. He said that he and Mr. Bill Tally needed neighbors like the two of them, men with sand in their makeup. You still had to protect your holdings from stray Indians and them damn sodbusters.

They appreciated it, but Red and Jug just had to see over the next hill. Cooped up all winter in a snowbound cabin was not for them. They had to answer this wandering yearning to discover new adventures.

They were up early and packed. Saying good-bye to these men, that they had gotten so close to over the hard trail, was best done quick. Mr. Dave settled up with them and was very generous. The cook had made Jug a big stack of those tortillas as a parting gift for his Tex-Mex friend. Once again, they promised to come by Cheyenne and visit them, but in their hearts they all knew that it was probably good-bye, forever. Rusty was ready to go and was tugging at the bit.

Chapter 21

After a week, they started seeing this cloudbank far ahead. After a couple of days, old Jug with his keen eyesight says, "Biggen, them ain't clouds. They ain't changing shape. You see that big peak with the white that looks like a big titty?"

They had caught their first glimpse of Pike's Peak. As they rode closer, it got bigger, a helluva lot bigger.

Red threw his head back to see the top and said, "Damn almighty! I never thought they were this big."

Jug was awed. Why the Appalachians were little molehills compared to these mountains.

This was a land of much bigger game, with a deer even bigger than the mule deer, called an elk and the grisly bear, which was said to be bigger than a horse and the meanest critter on earth. Why they even ate their own kind, if they caught a littler one not being protected by its mama. The Indians killed a few, but the bears kill a helluva lot more Indians. You had to get close with a bow and arrow and it a bunch of arrows to stop 'Old Eruphium', so they didn't fear man.

Jug had hung that forty-five-seventy Winchester on his horse along, with the one they had cabbaged on to when they shot those banditos. It was twice as powerful as their forty-five long Colts. Old crack shot Donley was ready. Bring on that bear and we'll make tortillas out of them buggers. They started climbing and looking for a pass through them mountains. You sure wasn't going over 'old baldy', that's the nickname they had given Pike's Peak. The lower slopes were timbered with big soft wooded pines. You could find dry wood for a fire in a short time. The grass in the open parts was rich and a horse was soon full and would put on weight if not ridden regularly. To top that off, the lakes were full of beaver and the prettiest rainbow trout that you have ever seen. Jug wanted to fish all the time. The trout were very tasty too.

The vistas were always changing and a little more awesome, so they almost looked like paintings. No wonder the Indians put up such a fight to keep their land. Red and Jug were told that in the far northwest, there were still small bands of renegade Indians in the mountains that fought a guerilla war and were almost impossible to wipe out. They liked to catch a couple of wanderers, like Red and Jug, and no one would be the wiser.

They heard Rusty snort one morning. Red and Jug were instantly awake and looking the way Rusty was pointing. They saw a big dun colored horse down by the lake, but brother this wasn't a horse, it was one of those big bears and he was cleaning up the fish heads that Jug had left there the evening before. He was glancing their way quite often and knew they were there. They stood there, watching him not fifty yards away, and after he finished eating, he turned and started walking their way.

Old Jug took a kneeling stance, his best shooting stance, and Red got ready too, but for some reason Jug was hesitatin' to fire.

Red finally said, "Little buddy, if you've got any reservations about firing old Big Bertha there, would you consider swapping guns with me?"

Red figured it would take all the cartridges in his rifle to stop that bear. He could shoot fast, but not that fast and the distance had done gotten too close. About that time Jug cut loose. That bear gave out the loudest roar you ever heard and stood up on his hind legs to see what dared to harm him. Red cut loose along with Jug. He was making a windmill out of that lever action rifle. You didn't have to aim it, just point and shoot. You might not hit the right spot, but you hit him. That bear wasn't twenty feet away when he give up the ghost. Damn almighty, Red was sweating. Shooting a man wasn't as bad as this.

He said aloud, "Little buddy, what was taking you so long to shoot?"

Jug said, "I wanted his head to quit swaying from side to side. I was trying for a headshot so I didn't shoot up his hide."

My word. Red was to learn that his little buddy was unpredictable about a lot of things.

Chapter 22

Fall had all ready come to the high country. They had seen magnificent vistas that went on and on, and that only God could have created. This was like the Garden of Eden and with little effort; you could live off the land. Living in these lofty peaks in all their grandeur would be enough to surely convince you that there was a Supreme Being. Red didn't believe the way that those fire and brimstone preachers, preached it. It seemed to Red that they all had a different take on it, to suit themselves. It's like the notches on his Colt. They certainly preached against that, but the courts hung people all the time that needed it. Red, in his way, did the same. He just didn't have time for the one's that needed killing to have a trial. What's the difference? The Indians worshiped a lot of different spirits, but most tribes believed in the Great Father that started it all.

They were headed for Santa Fe. It was the crossroads of several trading routes and it had a lot of comings and goings. Santa Fe had a mild climate and was on the foothills of the mountains. Also, there would be a lot of tortillas and frijoles. They could stay up with the news and fandangos of the Mexicans and the Pueblo Indians, all in the same place. They had bourbon from the States and rum from Mexico. They would winter there and then take the northern route over the mountains instead of straight across the desert to California. It was further, but prettier, and they had time to burn. They had heard about this Yellowstone country and all it's wonders.

They arrived in Santa Fe just in time; the winter had just closed the high passes. Santa Fe was really the crossroads of the west. Here, the American traders and teamsters, mixed with ox carts full of goods from Mexico. The Indians were in force also. Jug's Tex-Mex held them in good stead. He was teaching Red a smattering of that lingo, which might come in real handy in the future. Here a fortune could be made on one load of goods from St. Louis, if the timing was right. The wagons would leave the States as soon as the first green up, if they were to be in Santa Fe early and have the first goods there, to fetch high prices and then try to out trade the Mexicans for a load of hides to return with. It took strong men for this work and there was always friction between the different races that made up the population. A fellow had to watch his backside. It really helped to have a pard along; you covered each other.

It wasn't long before Jug had an Indian senorita warming his bed and cooking tortillas for him. The Indians spoke a mixture of Spanish and Indian and Jug fit right in. They figured they could live pretty well, as long as they made sure they saved enough for supplies the next spring. Anyways, all Jug needed was meal, coffee, some cartridges and them watered down rum drinks.

They listened everywhere they went and the only lead they heard was that some Taggerts in El Paso were looking for a Jim Sparks and were willing to pay money for any information. They had guessed right when they took the northern route, but the main northern trading routes run straight north to Santa Fe from El Paso. Red figured California would have the strongest draw on those Taggert nephews; they were living good on old Zeb's money. They would catch him sooner or later and later would suit the nephews just fine. They could pull it off, as long as they moved along and mailed reports back home, and got their next allowance. They had seen enough already to know that they would never bust another clod of that wore out clay soil back in Laurel, Mississippi.

Chapter 23

They had managed to stay out of trouble that winter in Santa Fe, but it had been close a couple times. There was a big change in plans, at the last minute. Jug had married that girl, Mary was her name, and now she was with child. It was agreed that Red would go north by himself and come back through there from California after seeing that big ocean that he desperately wanted to see. By then, Mary and the papoose would be able to travel, and they would maybe wander on up to Cheyenne and start ranching.

It wasn't easy, leaving Old Jug behind. He and Red were as close as brothers, but he was doing the right thing, and besides, Mary was very pretty and Jug liked her a helluva lot more that he put on. Red, Rusty and one packhorse left in late May. The passes were just now clearing of snow. Rusty and the pack mare were fat as butterballs, especially the mare. Why, Red was to find out later. If he thought that they had seen some pretty country, it was nothing compared to this Yellowstone country. He had quit going north and headed east. Red was in some very rugged mountains and he was wondering if that desert route wasn't the best after all. He saw some fresh Indian signs and swapped out his forty-five-caliber rifle for Big Bertha. Jug had insisted that he carry it and it would prove to be a wise move later on.

As Red climbed a high timbered ridge, he heard a dog barking. Was it Indians or white men? If it was Indians camped there, there should have been more than one. The Indians kept a lot of dogs in their main camps. First, because they were the camp scavengers and would eat anything, so that kept the camp clean. Some of the Indians ate the dogs too. An Indian's life was tough, but so was a dog's; double tough. Red dare not tie Rusty. You rode up and you didn't leave your horse. When he got closer, he realized he was approaching an Indian graveyard. They buried their dead up on scaffoldings and they were haunted places, so they lingered only long enough to get the job done. This lone dog was standing out in front of this dilapidated teepee. He would bark and then nervously look back inside. There was no one around, as far as Red could see. He dismounted, took his Colt out and eased up to that teepee for a look inside. He had already figured it out. When an Indian got real old or too crippled to travel and endangered the whole tribe, they brought them to a place like this, left about a weeks supply of food and water and left them to die. It seemed cruel, but the survival of the tribe came first.

This dog must have been a favorite pet and it just wasn't gonna yield. Red picked up a big stick, and it understood that well enough. The Indians give out harsh punishment to dogs. He ran off a little ways and quieted down. Red eased back the flap on that ragged teepee, no use to leave a good one, he may be able to use it anyways. The stench was terrible. Red thought they must have already died, but then he heard a faint moan. He went to one side and rolled up a couple feet of the tepee, to let in light and let some of that stench out.

He eased back inside and found an Indian girl. She was in terrible shape. She had been beaten nearly to death. She had been beaten on the head, had both arms broken, a leg broken and was so swollen about the face that she could only partly see. It was a miracle that she was alive. On looking further, Red could see there was a little new baby hanging to one teat. Her milk had long run dry but the baby was alive too. The stench was from the excrement they had been forced to wallowing in. Damn almighty.

He had heard about these things. Her husband had done this; she had been unfaithful to him. They usually just cut their wives through, but this one had tortured her and left them both to die a slow, agonizing death. It was probably a case of this young girl being in love with a buck her age and some older buck out bidding him to her folks, for her. She would be made to go live with his older wives and be assigned all the drudgery task. She ran away, but got caught. You can bet the younger buck was already dead.

Red set up his tent quickly in the valley floor, by a stream. They needed help fast if he was to save them. They were revolting to touch, but touch he must. He just slid her and the baby on that nasty bedroll down the hill. She had the look of a frightened doe on her face. There's no telling what she believed about white men. She moaned and Red knew to move at all was terrible for her. Red built a fire quickly and started heating water. He got some water and gave it to the girl. His mare had given birth to a colt several days before and he milked her, diluted the strong milk with water, and started spooning it in that baby's mouth, making sure that the mother could see what he was doing. He tried in his bad Spanish to tell the mother that he would help them.

He had warm water by then and he took all the wrapping off the baby and washed her up. She was in bad shape but was following him with her eyes, a good sign. He greased her little butt like he had seen the women do, wrapped her in a blanket and placed her in the tent. The dog seemed to understand and laid down close by.

This poor girl needed so much help it was hard to tell where to start, but the first thing he had to do was clean her up so he could stand to be close to her. All the while he was telling himself that if he ever came across the bastard that did this, he would try his best to kill him. He had to work slowly so as not to cause any more pain than necessary. She was moaning so, that he got some whiskey, watered it down, added some sugar, and stared spooning that to her. He gave her a pretty good shot and she quieted down. Red then took a couple of good shots himself and started washing her up. First the blood off her face, so she could see better. Everything went as smooth as could be, until he started on her bottom. She gave out a loud gasp; the embarrassment was great on both sides. He gave her some more whiskey and covered her face up. That seemed to help since she had to be cleaned. As Red touched her she would flinch, even after the whiskey, it hurt. He worked as fast as he could and was as gentle as he could be. He put her in the tent, on clean blankets, beside her baby. Next, he had to cook some stew to feed the mother. Damn almighty, what was he getting into now?

Chapter 24

While the stew was cooking, Red cut some small sticks for splints and wrapped her arms in soft fur. After he set them, as best he could, he then splinted them and wrapped them again, making slings for them both, so as not to move them any more than she had too. Thank God it was the lower leg, it would heal faster. He propped her up and fed her some thin stew. She finally lay back and dozed off. The papoose was fast asleep.

Red hadn't even tended to Rusty. He had wandered off to one side and was grazing. Red threw the dog a stew bone that had some meat on it and he attacked it savagely. He took off the packs and tied the horses on that good grass. Red sat down, drank some coffee and thought that he sure wished Jug was here. He could see a couple months anyways, before they could travel at best and their supplies would be running low by then. He could forget California this summer. A thought came to him like a bolt of lightning. He would name the girl Cher and the baby Leslie. He would pull them through. He knew he could. He didn't have to worry about the Indians coming back this year. They usually came back the following year, gathered up the bones that the varmints hadn't carried off and put them on a scaffold.

Leslie fussed and Red checked her diaper, but there was nothing there yet. He had thought about milking the mare, but he would just milk her as needed since she kept the milk warm. He was learning already, but he had a helluva lot more to learn before this summer was up. Off to the mare he would go, gets a cup full, cut it with water and spoon her a half cup. When she got where she could tolerate the straight stuff, she would grow like a weed on it. Yeah, buddy.

Red bought the horses in close. Next he made a toilet. He set a couple posts in the ground, tied a cross pole that was peeled smooth and about the right width, set two poles in front and hung a blanket in front of it. He didn't know how this would work out, but they had to try something. There was just not anything in the Indian culture to handle this. You just died or went to the river and relieved yourself. He then made himself a bed on the other side of the tent, as he would be awakened all through the night. Tomorrow he would fetch that old tepee. This small, two man tent just wasn't big enough for them in their condition. The Indian tepee was one of the best shelters ever made by man. Red could kill some elk and repair it and it would suit them just fine.

Chapter 25

The next morning, Red was up early with a warm fire out in front of the tent, and he opened the front up to let in the warmth. Cher had been awake and tossing and he suspected she needed to go to the toilet. He tried to sign to her, but no response. He thinks that if it wasn't for the baby, she would have crawled to the river and drowned herself. So, without further ado, he just picked her up in his arms and carried her out there to their makeshift toilet and sat her on that log. Red turned his back and walked away several yards to give her even more privacy, but he could see under that blanket. He had left it off the ground just for that purpose. When he knew she was through, he went back and carried her back inside and laid her on her bed, as gently as he could. Then he tended to Miz Leslie, the little heifer was crying, but that was a good sign. He stirred up some bread. This was more like Indian bread than any other kind. He baked the bottom for a bit, then propped it up, facing the fire and browned the top. He warmed up the stew, changed the baby's diaper and went after milk. He spooned that mare's milk in Miz. Leslie until she didn't want any more and she nodded off. He watered the horses, and then staked Rusty on good grass. Red kept the mare close since he was going to use her nibs to fetch that tepee.

Next, he fed Cher and himself. Her face was better. She couldn't have been more than eighteen or so, and if both sides looked like the side that wasn't beat up; she was quite pretty. She was tall and slim and that was a blessing with her broken limbs. He couldn't begin to guess what tribe she was from. She wouldn't try to talk but could sign. This was going to be a challenge. Yeah, buddy.

He cut some poles, made a travois for the mare and went after that tepee. Friend, the old buffalo hides on a regular tepee are heavy, but them old squaws on moving day can have one loaded and ready to go in a few minutes. Red got it back down and starts putting up the poles. He wished he hadn't been so fast and had paid more attention to the way they went. He was about worn out.

He had left the tent open and finally, there came a stream of jabber from Cher. She could speak broken Mexican and he could understand most of it. Boy howdy, that was a big help. She told him how to do it and he had it up in no time. He moved them inside and built a fire in the middle. This was a lot more roomy and you could see Cher perk up; it was her tepee. Best of all, she could tell him when she hurt and needed to make a toilet run. She could also interpret the baby's wants a lot better than he could.

She told him that the dog was her pet from a puppy and how she found him, up there by that graveyard, one night. He stood off several wolves for the longest. He liked to come in and lay by her and nuzzle Leslie. He was smart, even if he didn't look like nothing, with a medium build, dark red colored and with a long sharp muzzle. He had a long tail that curled over his back. He soon accepted Red and wouldn't bother anything left out, like food or hides. Red made himself a papoose cradle, put back straps on it, stuffed Leslie in it and carried her around. The mountain men called it going 'Indian.'

Well, he didn't have a choice, it seemed. He even carried her on a short hunt one day. She would ride back there, giggling and baby cooing, but the minute he saw game and tensed up and started stalking it, her natural instincts told her to be quiet. It was uncanny. He was sure getting attached to this little papoose. She would cry for him instead of Cher and Cher would mimic a pout, but she was glad that this big redheaded man had come into their lives.

Chapter 26

Cher was moving about now on some crutches. She could put some pressure on her armpits. Red had put much smaller wrappings and splints on her arms now. She could hobble and hop to the toilet and balance Leslie on her lap for a while. She crawled a lot and she would crawl to the stream and partly bathe herself. This was a great help to Red. Red could see she wasn't lazy and was determined to do for herself. Their supplies were getting low and they must be gone soon.

Red was beginning to enjoy his family. Cher's face had completely healed now and she was very pretty. He found that he was enjoying their touching when necessary and he sensed that she did too. He found himself shaving more often, changing into clean clothes and cooking her favorite meals. Leslie was growing fat on that rich mare's milk. The colt seemed drawn to Leslie and Red guessed it could smell it's mother's milk on her. He always looked forward to combing Cher's jet back hair and plating it in two long braids . He was sure he sensed a stirring in her when they were close and the tables were turned this time. Here was a woman that he wanted and he was sure he knew how to make that happen.

A few days later, as he approached camp, he heard the dog having a tizz. Red spurred Rusty on and as he got closer, he heard Cher let out a blood curdling scream There, standing over Cher, was a big buck Indian. He was about to stab her with a long knife. The big rifle came up and Red fired. The big bullet caught the Indian in the chest before he could do his dirty work. Another Indian ran from the tepee and Red dropped him too. He ran to Cher and held her to calm her down. The big buck was still twitching, so Red pulled his Colt and emptied it into him. He was Cher's former husband and the man that had hurt her. He had come back to claim her bones and found her alive. There were three of them, but one got away and he would spread the alarm. They would have to leave their little valley, this day.

Red tied the mare to the two bodies and drug them off, before Cher could calm down. He made a travois for the mare, packed up the tepee and tent with what supplies they had left, and slung Leslie on one side of the packsaddle on the mare. He put Cher up behind him and they headed south. They could be easily followed now, but by the time that third buck got back to camp, told what had happened and the medicine man figured out if she really was alive or a sprit, they had a little time. Red was also hoping the spirits would be good to them and bring rain to wash out any trace of their trail. They had to push on toward Santa Fe. Would old Jug be surprised to see Red's family. Jug didn't have nothing on old Red no more.

He even got his French harp out and played *Dixie*. Leslie liked that. They rode into Santa Fe and were hardly noticed. The natives were used to strange sights here, but Cher and Leslie were all eyes. They made their way to Jug's adobe house and were hugged and slapped on the back to no end. They would winter over and head for Cheyenne in the spring. Ever since they started traveling, Cher and the baby shared Red's bed. Cher was his, so he just held her close. There was a lifetime of loving ahead of them. Red added two more notches to his Colt, for the ones that he had killed that needed it.

Chapter 27

Jug and Red had started gathering up the supplies that they would need to start a ranch and raise their families in Cheyenne. They were gonna go and look up Mr. Bill Tally and all their other old pards on the Lazy Bar Eight. They wanted to take them up on their offer to help them get started in the ranching business. They had already named their outfit and had their branding irons made. It was to be called The Rockin' Jug, with a jug sitting on a rocker.

Jug and Mary had a chubby boy born that spring they named Bar and Red's Cher was with child. Damn almighty, they were gonna need help and the best way to get it, seemed to raise it. This wasn't gonna be any work yourself to death ranch. Red and Jug was gonna still roam those high mountains, hunt and fish and take the wife and children with them because those longhorn cows take care of themselves all summer. They had bought a couple rolls of this new barbed wire to put around their corn patch. They bought two grindstones and planned to build a gristmill on one of those mountain streams and grind their own cornmeal. Jug had to have those tortillas and beans. Mr. Dave, their old boss, had already told them that beans grew good in that rocky bottom land.

They would each have a covered wagon, the two pack mares and that one-year-old colt that was born where Red found Cher and Leslie. Of course, Red's Rusty and Jug's saddle horse too. Leslie was toddling now. They would set her out in front of the tepee, where they lived on the edge of town, and Old Mutt, as Red named that dog, would lay by her and nothing was gonna bother her. The only thing he would let approach her was that colt. Red thought that colt thought Leslie was his sister, but just looked different. Red had already promised the colt to her. She would have a trusted companion for many years that might pay off big time one day. The colt was longer legged than most, so they called him Tallboy.

They pulled out as soon as the spring weather would permit. The went east on the freight road by Chimney Rock. They would come out at Pueblo, follow the east range and stay on the prairie all the way to Cheyenne. They were using four-up teams of horses, as they were faster and this trip shouldn't be that tough. Those horses would be cow ponies till they raised some mountain horses. Cheyenne was in the lower part of Wyoming and wasn't that far. They could make it and have time to build Jug and Mary a cabin. Red and Cher would live in that tepee the first winter. It suited them just fine. Red had replaced most of the old hide in it with new steer hides. Cher had showed him how to tan the hides, and then smoke them so they stayed waterproof and soft.

Having a pretty squaw for a wife definitely had its advantages when you lived on the frontier. They didn't fuss back at you like white women, were hardy, weren't hardly ever sick, and never complained about the heat and cold. Red had taught Cher how to shoot and she and Leslie liked to accompany him on hunting trips. She would be all right if a panther or bear came around the tepee while he was out on the range. Red and Jug had picked them up another one of those Big Bertha rifles, so they figured that now in a fight, they would out gun most.

They had stopped in Cheyenne and inquired about The Lazy Eight and were told that it was in a big valley, about forty miles on north. Two more days of pushing, long days, and they would be there. They were anxious to see their pards and Jug wanted to show the cook that baby boy.

Chapter 28

As they were approaching The Lazy Eight, a couple outriders saw them coming and headed them off. They were gonna warn the sodbusters off their land. It turned out to be J. T. Anderson and Bob Kajar. John Thomas sent Bob back to the ranch headquarters with the news. Mr. Dave and nearly the whole outfit came riding, hell bent for leather, shooting off their six-shooters. They had really never thought this day would happen. They bought the springboard wagon and insisted on the womenfolk being brought on in it. The cowboys would take over the wagon and teams. Mr. Bill Tally told the cook to barbecue a steer, lots of beans and trimmings. They were gonna have a fiesta.

The President couldn't have gotten a better welcome. Several of the boys had wives that lived a few miles away and this was a big outfit. They were running ten thousand head now. They all came in. Miz Tally was the sweetest woman, near saintly. Mr. Bill said there was this well watered valley just over a log range of mountains, fifteen miles further north, that he was already running a thousand head on. That would be their start and not to think about paying, until they could sell their increase in a couple years.

Their friends demanded that the stay around a week or so and tell them all the news and hear their stories. Then they would send some of the boys to help them each build a ranch house. He said that since they were ranchers now, to stop calling him Mr. Dave. They were neighbors and from now on he was just Dave. That cook cried when he saw Jug. It was like a son coming home. Jug cut loose with his Pueblo Spanish and old Nunez, the cook, hugged him some more.

Chapter 29

It had been fifteen years since Jug and Red had first come to Squaw Valley and started the Rockin' Jug Ranch. They raised longhorn cattle and kids. They had started with a thousand head and built it up to five thousand head. Not as big a spread as some went, but they only wanted a good living. Jug or Red, neither one had any ambition to be rich and powerful. Bill Tally was running ten thousand or more and had gotten quite rich and was a man to be reckoned with around The Cattlemen's Association.

Each spring The Rockin' Jug threw in with The Lazy Eight, about two thousand head each, which was their normal increase per year, and drove them to the rail head at Dodge City. Red had bought some shorthorn bulls and started upgrading the herd. The Shorthorn cross would flesh out more and mature in half the normal five years it took a Longhorn. They got the best of both breeds; a more trackable cow with the hardness of the Longhorn and more tender and fleshy like the Shorthorn.

The other thing they were good at was raising kids. Red and Cher had four girls and Jug and Mary had four boys. Red finally figured he would just have to do what his Cousin Jack did, back in Louisiana on Bayou Bodcau. He'd keep those girls close and use those strong son-in-laws as hands, so what's the difference? First there was the full-blooded Leslie, a dead ringer of her mother, tall and beautiful. Next was Donna, the only redhead, who was very sweet to a point and then could kill in an instant, if one needed it. Christi was a strawberry blond, but had the tawny skin and was more serious. Then there was the last, Mandylou. She was named after Red's Aunt Barb, a big talker. Red was told that's where he got all his blathering from and Mandy had come into the world yelling and hadn't stopped since.

Old Jug had all boys. The first born, Bar, was the meanest little fart you ever did see and Jug spoiled him. Then came Randy, Doc and Frank. Bar took after Jug, but was chubby and the others showed that dominant squaw blood. The Lazy Eight had some married hands and there were suitors to go around, but Red was proud of his pretty girls. They were taught to ride at an early age. Red took them hunting and fishing at an early age too. He taught them to shoot and told them not to trust strangers and to always stand their ground. He instilled in them that the Chandler's didn't run from a fight. They each had their own pistol and knew how to use it, so not to hesitate and get killed mulling over a challenge too long.

Red and Jug had filed on their homesteads and the two of them just about covered the best water in their valley. Then, as they made money, they bought up the adjoining land until they were pretty safe from the land grabbers. They would find a settled ranch and hire some misfits to come in and homestead off parcels of the best farmland and then sell it to the immigrants coming west.

Bill Tally had filed on his homestead, then had his hands do the same, but his place was so vast that the owned portion was small in comparison to what he claimed. He wasn't gonna pay anybody any money for land that he reckoned wasn't his. By God, he had fought the Indians and the rustlers for that land and be damned if the sodbusters and land grabbers were gonna have it.

The range wars had started. The first act was to just burn them out, and then real intimidation started, by killing one of them. Jug and Red were drug into this on Bill's side. After all, they would never have been ranchers if it hadn't been for Bill. This, Bill had seen coming and he had got them in his debt, way back. Red and Jug really didn't have any stomach for this kind of killing. Killing them that needed it was a helluva lot different than killing a poor farmer that had struggled and give up everything he had to come out here and make a new start. These were innocent farmers and they had a legal right to homestead this government land that was just claimed by the cattle barons.

Of course, the big stockmen had the ear of the Governor at first, until the sodbusters got the upper hand in voting numbers, then the politicians started changing quickly. There's nothing that will make a politician flip-flop as quick as a voting majority, right or wrong.

The stockmen were an independent lot and tough as nails. They rose up in anger, formed the Cattlemen's Association and hired outlaw gunmen to do their dirty work. Red tried to talk some sense into them, but was shouted down. In the end, The Lazy Eight and The Rockin' Jug weren't friends anymore. It was the worst of times. It reminded Red of the Civil War. The rich man's war and the poor man's war. Brother against brother and friend against friend.

It would have went on forever it seemed, but for the winter of eighty-eight and eighty-nine. They had two of the coldest winters ever, in a row. It wiped out whole herds. The big open valley of The Lazy Eight was devastated. The Rockin' Jug was broken up with a lot more badlands, so their cattle could hide from that killing sub-zero wind in the breaks and they only lost half their herd. A lot of outfits along with the sodbusters just folded up and left the country.

The Lazy Eight was one of them. Bill Tally was one of them. He had too much pride and bitterness to let Jug and Red help him and they heard later that he died a bitter and broken man.

Chapter 30

It was taking a while to bounce back from the killing winters of eighty-eight and eighty-nine. Word was in Cheyenne, that if anybody could make it, them damn squaw men up there in Squaw Valley, so named after Red and Jug, could make it.

The girls came to realize that their daddy had a past. It had been years since they had even heard of them Taggerts, but Red knew that a man like Zeb Taggert would never give up and as he got older Red's paranoia would get the best of him sometimes. He had whirled and drawn on his Leslie, as she could slip around like a ghost at times. She learned better and came to realize the danger of it and how upsetting it was to her daddy. About twice a year Red and Jug would team up, carry a jug out to a line cabin on the high north rim, and stay about a week, getting rip roaring drunk. They forbid anyone else to come near.

To prove their point, Christi came to see them and carried a message. Before she got very close, they started bouncing bullets off of the rocks around her and she high tailed it out of there. She went back to the ranch and told her mama that her daddy and Uncle Jug were drunken crazy up there on that little lake, just under Judge Bryant Peak. From then on it was referred to as 'Crazy Lake'.

Red was drunk up there, but he and Jug would never really endanger those girls. They could drink enough to be melancholy and mean, but Red knew that some day there would come a time when those Taggerts were sure to show up and he might lose, so he wanted to teach those girls to stand on their own and to not depend on their daddy to make their decisions.

Red taught the girls to read and they could speak Indian, Tex-Mex Spanish, as well as English with a far northwest accent. Leslie and Donna liked to visit the Indian reservation and stay among them for several days at a time. They were safe, as they were armed and besides,

Red gave them beaves a couple times a year when they had the big Sun Dance and the Winter Moon Dance. He was known among the Indians as Chief Diablo, The Red Devil.

Leslie and Christi would get many admiring glances from the young bucks and they delighted in flirting with them. One young buck got so carried away that he came calling on Christi at the ranch. Decorum demanded that they treat him as an equal, that's the way of the tribe; to slight him would have ruined their relationship on the whole reservation. Most whites said the Indians were sullen. Hell, don't you think the Romans thought the same thing about the Jews that took their land.

The Indians were a stone culture that ran head on in to an iron culture and it was inevitable who would win. Their birth rates, in normal times, were equal to their dying rate. This kept them from over populating themselves. The Indians talked like they were the only ones that took care of the land and game. The Indians killed a lot of buffalo sometimes and lived from feast to starvation. Also, the big tribes were in flux and killing out or pushing out the weaker tribes, a thousand years or more before the white man came. They had slaves captured in war and to be a slave of a hunter was a tough life indeed, but to lose their beautiful mountains, with the hunting and roaming as they pleased, was a hard pill to swallow. The bitterness will never completely go away. The South took a licking that will last in the southerner's mind for many years. It is said in the land where the Lord lived that the Jew and Arab are still carrying old grudges from way back then.

Red wasn't prejudice but he didn't want any reservation buck hanging around. He was educating his daughters. He ordered a variety of books from back east and the girls would meet the stage and pick them up. Leslie would cause quite a stir amongst those stage riders. She would dress up in her Indian finery, wait behind Lookout Rock, and as the stage came up, dash out in front of it.

Old man Ray Burleigh, the driver, would catch a glimpse of her and would act surprised. It wouldn't do to completely surprise Mr. Ray because these were still rough times.

He would set them horses back on their heels and holler, "Everyone be calm! We can talk our way out of this."

He would sigh and then say, "Oh, it's just Princess Blue Bird, wanting her books."

Needless to say, this pretty girl sitting astride her fancy long-legged pony Tallboy, wasn't anything like the stories that most had been led to believe about Indians. A lot of young men were hardly the same for months after seeing her beauty. Oh, she always had her pistol and her rifle was in its scabbard. They were for real. Yeah, buddy.

The day Tallboy saved her life, she was returning from a visit on the reservation, and two renegade bucks of the worse sort followed her. They were gonna have their way with her. They really wanted her fancy pistol and rifle. They were almost up with her before she discovered them. When they were found out, they charged her, giving war whoops to try and frighten her horse and build up their courage. Leslie spurred Tallboy and the race was on, but their horses didn't stand a chance with Tallboy. As she drew away, they started shooting at her. They had planned to kill her under any circumstances, even if they didn't catch her; the fat was in the fire. They would be banned from the tribe forever, if Red didn't catch them first.

Leslie was soon far enough ahead that she was out of sight and could dash behind a rock.

She remembered her daddy saying, "We Chandlers don't run from a fight, if we are armed."

She whirled around and hid and as they swooped by, she would just wing one of them and teach them a lesson. But damn, she missed his arm and got a solid body hit. She knew he was dead by the time he hit the ground and he landed in a rolling heap. Damn almighty, she couldn't let the other one get away and spread lies, so at long range, she got him too. She drug their bodies up to a narrow arroyo and rolled them in. She threw some tumbleweed in after them, so as not to attract vultures, caught their horses and turned them loose. They would join the wild herd; they wouldn't go back to the reservation, as the tribe had used these horses hard.

The wind and sand would soon hide their tracks and she was pretty sure that they hadn't told anyone what they were up to. Like she had heard Daddy say, killing wasn't so bad if the ones you killed, needed it. She would do a bunch one day. She didn't tell anyone. Daddy had told them how some bad men had got their name and anyone trying to bother them could be under the Taggert's hire, to get back at him.

Chapter 31

Cher had remembered that she had an Aunt Margo, the wolf woman that lived on the edge of the Black Hills, and she wanted to see her people again. Aunt Margo was a Metz, that's what they called the half French, half Indian breed. Margo's daddy, Randy Cheramie, was a French Voirger, a trapper working for The Hudson Bay Company. He had been killed while trapping beaver in the high mountains and Margo had stayed with her people. Maybe she would know where Cher's mother and father were. When they all gathered for the Sun Dance, held on Bear Mountain in the scared Black Hills each year, she would ask.

So the next summer Red, Cher, and all the girls headed on a pilgrimage to try and find their lost kin. Red and the girls tanned some cowhides, cut some lodge poles and Cher taught them how to make another tepee. It was soon done, for this was high adventure for the girls and they really got into the task. They wouldn't pull it with a travois, but carried it on a light wagon. They would live sparsely and hunt and fish all along the way. Leaving everything at the ranch in Jug and the boys' hands, they set out. They were expecting to be gone all summer. Red made them bring books, since he wasn't gonna let them go "all injun", as they called it.

The girls were as happy as larks. Red and Cher were just kind of along for the ride, or so it seemed at times. The girls did all the chores, hunted and fished. Who needed them stubborn boys anyways? Red figured his girls were tougher than most, with the reedman's genes coursing through their veins. These crossbreeds had the best of both men's genes. It had long been known, back in the settlements, that to cross a setter with a pointer bird dog would get you a superior dog known just as a Drop.

This was known as some of the most beautiful country and it was full of game. The Indians held The Black Hills sacred. They made hunting trips there, got lodge poles for their tepees, but then went back out on the plains to camp. Some kept close to the fringe of them.

They timed their visit to get there just ahead of the Sun Dance ceremony. This was about the most important ceremony of all to the tribes, everywhere. They asked about Cher's people and were told that some would be there. They had heard of the legend of the girl and her baby that were left to die at the burying place, twenty summers ago. How their faithful dog turned into a man and had killed her husband and his brother when they had returned to claim the bones. The tribe was so scared of that place they refused to ever go there again.

The found Aunt Margo and at first she wouldn't believe it, but this was a tough old girl and being a breed, she didn't have as nearly a closed mind as the full bloods on these things. She said nearly all her mother's tribe had died from the awful white man's sickness, the Pox, and they were no more. Maybe it was meant to be, that she was blessed after all. Cher and Leslie had gone white and Red had gone Indian. They had met in the middle and what a wonder full life it had been, except for that dark cloud that would always hang over Red.

Chapter 32

The girls were very independent and they were getting to a very marriageable age, but most of their exposure had been to Jug's boys, especially after the range wars. To top it off, they were so close to Jug's boys that they seemed like brothers and sisters. Another thing was that Red always had something of interest going on, hunting and fishing trips to new places, to just working on the ranch. They feared also, that the day would come when the Taggert gang would come and they would be needed. If something happened to their Mama and Daddy, they wouldn't forgive themselves.

Those two outlaws had told one more person back on the reservation about their plan to bushwhack Leslie that day and how they were now missing. Their horses were found running with the wild herd. The U.S. Marshall's were notified in Denver. It was one thing for the government to break all their treaties and keep the Indians nearly starving on a reservation, but lo to any civilian to touch one.

They issued a warrant for Leslie's arrest. They had to have an inquiry. They would take Red's word for it, that he would bring her to Denver himself on the appointed day. Well, they figured they didn't have any other choice. It would take a small army to take this young lady in. They weren't fools. When an upstanding rancher gave you his word, it was law and you could count on it, albeit that he was a squaw man.

Leslie had never told any one about that day. For one thing, she didn't want her Daddy worrying about that too. Red figured there was a damn good chance that she had shot them. As he remembered, it seemed that Cher told him that Leslie had been quiet for a couple days after that visit, but he wasn't gonna ask because he really didn't want to know. They didn't have a case, but you could never tell, these government types were mostly appointed political sops. They needed to look good for the reporters from back east and to win a civil rights case was a sure fire way to get promoted. You could bet one thing, there would be a lot more killing before they got his first-born; the one that he had saved from starvation by probably just one day.

The whole bunch loaded up, the Donleys and all the Chandlers and they were heavily armed. They quietly kept them under blankets in the wagon. But just in case, Red hired the slickest mouthpiece in the whole western district, Chuck Sawlow. It was said that he could make a witness forget his name and a lot of them to break down and cry and say they had forgotten everything. He told Red that the government didn't have a chance, as it was all hinged on a renegade buck's word and that he wouldn't risk coming. He was guilty himself of rustling The Rockin' Jug's cattle or would be when good old Chuck got through with him. Mr. Chuck had asked around to the effect, if Running Bear was a rustler and Running Bear took off and was hiding in the Mountains. Mr. Chuck was good but expensive and this rankled Red no end.

There was one hurdle they had to be careful of, and that was old Judge Bryant. Judge J.H. Bryant was pro-government and almost always ruled in the government's favor. It could go bad in many ways. Denver wasn't much of a town in those days and the hearing was held in the old American Fur trading post. The day of the hearing, The Rockin' Jug folks were there early and got the front seats. They were a serious bunch and they wanted the government's sops to know that. The government had a tribal spokesman there and he got up and gave an account of what they thought happened that day. When old slick Chuck got through with him, he admitted it was all hearsay, even with Judge Bryant cutting him off every way he could.

The government prosecutor even used Spanish when he wanted to convey a message to the judge. It was allowed, but Jug interpreted for them and got a way with it. Then Leslie was called. The fat prosecutor was used to having these local Indians for lunch, but was he surprised. This squaw girl was as smart as he was. You bet he wasn't gonna get anything out of this stubborn full blood that she didn't want to tell him.

One Indian trick was to just look puzzled and go mute. Then the hearing was over. They could prod, shout and threaten, but to no use. Mr. Chuck had told her that when it had gone on long enough, he would raise his voice and an objection and then she was to go mute. Then all the Judge could do was rule.

The Feds realized this showcase trial was over. The judge declared he would rule in a couple hours. To win was big, but to lose and be caught in a flat out lie, was scandalous. Even worse for the government, this would reverberate all the way back to Washington and if you put any of the real biggies in a stew, your career was finished. The judge's ruling was for dismissal, but it galled him. You could bet that he would be watching this bunch and they better not be guilty of a federal crime and be in front of him again. It would be many years before the Indian would begin to get a fair shake.

Chapter 33

A bunch of promoters started finding big ranches and selling them to foreigners, mostly wealthy British investors. They wanted to get rich quick in the cattle business, and prance around back home. They also wanted to come out west and hunt the plentiful game. They bought The Lazy Eight from the Denver bank and bought five thousand head of two-year-old steers. They would run them two years and then dump them on the market. They did this every year until they were running twenty thousand head. This was happening all over and in about five years, the market would be overstocked and another big bust was coming.

Meanwhile, they wanted to roam the mountains and hunt and fish the unspoiled spots. They were soon pointed towards The Rockin' Jug ranch. Jug and Red had just what they were looking for. They were generous spenders and they wanted to travel in style. Jug's sons, Randy, Doc and Frank, went as the camp keepers and wagon drivers. Mandylou and Donna were cooks. Those Englishmen asked a lot of questions and that was right down Mandy's road. She talked all the time anyways, but the heifer could make a nut cake that was out of this world. Donna prepared the game and Cher had taught her how to cook primitively, over an open fire. Red and Jug were the guides. This was great adventure for them; they were getting paid for it too.

Bar, the oldest of Jugs sons, stayed home to run the ranch. As the eldest, he was being groomed to take over the ranch anyways. Leslie was to act as protector. Red knew she had the sand for the job and knew to watch for any Taggerts. Christi was to help with her mother.

They were gone half the year. They went all the way to the Oregon Coast.

Red got to see the ocean, with its big waves, that went racing to be first to bash against the big rocks, be shoot high in the air as froth, then fall back and go back were waves come from and get in line to do it again.

This was one of the things Red had dreamed of seeing on that long ago trip, when he had discovered Cher and Leslie. He felt his life was complete now. It was unknown to Red, but their reputation as guides was growing. They were hired by another bunch for the next summer, to take out a group of Americans from the East. One of them that stood out was a medium sized fellow that was the most enthusiastic man that Red ever did see. He was very wealthy but liked to rough it. He was into politics and was even mentioned as running for President of the States. He, Red and Jug hit it off big, right from the start. Jug said that if this guy, T. R. as his friends called him, ever did that, Red would start voting and give him his vote.

Red and Jug were getting a little long in the tooth for men that had been rode hard and put away wet, many times. You were old at fifty. Most old cowboys were beat up from getting kicked and run over by the wild cows. They usually started at about fifteen years old, but every now and again you might find a cowboy that was only ten. Then those tough horses took their toll also. Things were coming together pretty good. Leslie had married Bar Donley. He would inherit Jug's part and Leslie would have Red's. The other kids were given the equivalent in money, as their part. The main thing in the west was to keep the ranch together and keep the family name going. Wasn't always fair to some of the kids, but that's just they it was.

Jug and Red had gotten where they went up to Crazy Lake and pulled their big drunk more often. They had remained inseparable pards and could spend hours in each other's company. They felt like they had done a good job for two outlaws and shooters of yesteryear.

Chapter 34

Things had been quiet for a while. Mandylou had met and married a businessman from Cheyenne, a young Irishman by the name of David Owens. He was a die-hard hunter. He got to know Frank Donley and started coming up to The Rockin' Jug and the rest is history. Red knew it had to be; they couldn't all stay on the ranch forever. Best of all, David was a good listener and being married to Mandylou, he was gonna need to be, [You bet]. Damn almighty, she could rattle on. Cher said she was just like him. My Word.

A disgruntled cowboy that had worked for The Lazy Eight and had lost his job in the big winters of eighty-eight and eighty-nine, was still blaming the bust on Red and Jug, for not going along in the range wars. He would badmouth them to anyone around. He had drifted on down to Dodge City and turned into a ne'er-do-well. Three eastern type fellows were in town, showing a flyer and offering a reward to anyone that could give them a line on Jim Sparks.

This Judas was being shown the picture and instantly recognized Red Chandler. When they described him as a big redhead, he was sure of it. He told them that he would come to their hotel room, since he was sure that he knew their man. He slipped in the back way of the hotel after dark that night. He couldn't be seen, as The Rockin' Jug was held in high esteem in Dodge, and in this day, a snitch would be in real trouble. Hell, he had heard that if Red or Jug didn't get you, them tough breed girls would. Damn, almighty.

D. Stewart would live to rue this day. He sensed these fellows would pay double for this information and it wasn't too hard to get them to agree. They were at the end of their rope. They were tired of roaming and that was the only way Zeb Taggert would keep the money coming. Shelling out that money all the time, made a money hungry man like Zeb Taggert even more bitter. He had figured out long ago the true story of Red and Cher's love affair and the intentional killing of Leslie by his jealous sons, but no matter. He would make that cane breaker pay the ultimate price. In truth, he had lost all four of his sons. Out of the ones that ran that day, one had committed suicide and the other was a helpless alcoholic.

Stewart told the three Taggert cousins that the man they were really looking for was Red Chandler, a rancher that lived in Squaw Valley. He was married to a full-blooded Indian and had a bunch of breed children. Stewart told them how to get there and the set up on the ranch. Stewart said he was damn sure that was their man. Old Red had a past and lots of folks knew that he was a hunted man.

He told them to just wait a couple days. The Cheyenne Fat Stock Show and Rodeo was opening and the whole bunch would be there. They gave Stewart his money and started laying plans to get their man. With Red's popularity and kin, they would never be able to take him alive. They would just shoot him and run. It was surely to be in all the papers. They could get one in St. Louis, to show Uncle Zeb, collect their bonus and settle down. The fair opened and the whole Rockin' Jug clan was there, except Cher and Red. The Taggerts cornered their man and he told them that Red and his wife would be there in the middle of the week. This big to-do would go on all week.

CHAPTER 35

The Taggerts figured that the easy way to get Chandler would be to get him on the road, close to the ranch, then hightail it out of there. They would have a four-day start. They would get him on a Wednesday, go to Denver, catch a train to St. Louis and then to New Orleans, Louisiana, where Uncle Zeb was now. Uncle Zeb was soon to be the Governor and with his power as Governor of the state, they were safe.

They rode out to the ranch and followed a timbered ridge that was close to the back of the ranch. They stopped, set their horses and used a spyglass to check it out. There was smoke coming out of the chimney, so someone was home. Jug Donley's house looked dead. This should be easy. Cher asked Red to bring some onions from the garden out back. There were two things that were the last thing Red always did before he stepped out the door and that was pick up his Colt and put on his hat. Today he did neither. As Red was getting those onions, the Taggert cousins rode the short distance to the house. One guarding the front and the other took one side. They rode to the garden. As Red straightened up, he saw instantly that he was trapped and didn't have a chance. He started a slow walk to the house. These two already had their guns out. He had always wondered how it would be.

Cher had caught a glimpse of the riders and sensed danger. She grabbed up Red's Colt and started running to him. Red started shouting for her to go back. He knew it was too late for him and he didn't want her to be caught in the gunfire. They shot him down; didn't give him a chance. They let Cher reach him, but it was too late for any words. As she bent over him, they killed her too. Then, as proof to Uncle Zeb, they cut off one of Red's hands. The papers were sure to mention that. They would pickle it and get that bonus. They turned their horses toward Denver and The Missouri Pacific passenger train to St. Louis. They would toast a job well done, at last.

A cowboy came to Leslie and told her that a ne'er do well was drunk, flashing a roll and bragging about sicking those Taggerts on Red Chandler. She rounded up Jug. He and his sons drug the drunk out in a back alley and started kicking him around. Leslie had heard enough. She mounted up and started back to the ranch. She rode hard. It was getting late and the ranch was dark when she got there. She quickly dismounted, drew her pistol and started calling her mother. She found the back door open, stepped out and saw them by the garden gate. She could tell by the way they were sprawled that it was too late. Her pain was indescribable. She got some blankets to lay them on and cover them with. That's when she discovered her daddy's hand missing.

She made a solemn vow that the Taggerts would be the hunted now, and she would show them what a squaw could do when she really hated someone. It wasn't long until the others all came in. They had made the drunk talk, and then they cut his throat and turned him loose. He staggered twenty feet, trying to scream.

PART II

Chapter 36

They buried their mother and father at Crazy Lake, under the tall ponderosa pines in a park like setting, where you could get a wide view of Squaw Valley. The whole family was making some kind of plans for revenge. They could partly understand how that rich white man may have felt toward their Daddy, but to kill their mother and mutilate their Daddy, demanded revenge. Not anything as simple as just shooting, either. They would count coup before they killed them.

Leslie moved into the old tepee up by Crazy Lake and for a week, fasted and prayed to the Great Eagle to guide her and give her a plan. On the last day, the Great Eagle lit in a tall pine and told her that she and Donna were to take up the trail, as they were the oldest. They would find the enemy in a big city, by the ocean. There were four of them and they would be very cunning, but two women could count coup on this enemy. This was the best way, as they had a weakness for women. They should keep her brothers and sisters away, since they could best work alone.

Leslie came from her dreamtime and called her sisters, Jug, and his boys together. She repeated what the Great Eagle had told her, that Jug and the boys were not to get involved, as this was a Chandler debt. The Great Eagle told her that it had given her strong medicine to be victorious and He would guide her and Donna as they walked in that strange other world. At first, the Donleys wouldn't hear of it, but Miz Donley, the other full-blood in the family, told them that the Great Sprit had spoken and that they must abide by His advice if Donna and Leslie were to have victory.

Leslie knew where to find the Taggerts, it wouldn't be a long hunt. The tricky part was to count coup and not get caught or draw suspicion to herself and Donna. It may take a lot of time and planning, but she had the rest of her life. She would not only show them that they were hunted, but by whom. If her planning was right, they would know right before she counted coup.

She and Donna would catch a train from Denver to St. Louis, where they would buy city clothes, some wigs and then catch a steamboat to Vicksburg, Mississippi. Once there, she would take a train east to Meridian, Mississippi to the three cousins' home and catch them first. Donna would go on to New Orleans and wait for her. She would rent a house in the city and set herself up as Miz Cher Pluisant. They were coming full circle and this circle was a noose tightening around the Taggert's necks.

Leslie cut her long black hair and got her a curly wig so she would pass as a Creole lady with means, or a pretty high yeller, to them Taggert boys. She wasn't in Meridian long, before she found out that one of the cousins Clay, had came straight home. He asked a prominent merchant's daughter to marry him and now that he had money. They were to leave the next day for New Orleans, with her mother as chaperone. Leslie made sure that she was on that train. They normally wouldn't associate with a pretty Creole, even one of means, but she could travel in the same club car with them.

Clay had been without a woman for several weeks now. He had gotten to like the Mexican girls of the Southwest and here was a fiery Creole. She was giving him sly glances, so he bribed the porter for the use of another Pullman berth. He excused himself and walked toward Leslie. She gave him a smile, rolled her eyes for him to follow her, and walked from one coach to the next to wait on him. He would price her. Money was no object and in any case, it couldn't be too high. The little connecting walkway was close. As he smelled her perfume, she could tell that he was already excited.

To start the conservation, he said, "Who are you, do you live around here?"

Leslie stuck her Derringer in his soft belly and said, "I am Leslie Chandler."

Clay said, "You're what?" He then looked like he was crapping in his pants.

She said, "You will never have enough money to buy me and where you are going you ain't gonna need nothing."

Then she shot him two times in the belly with them forty-one flatnosed slugs. Real gut wrenchers that the gamblers carried for their under the table gun, if they caught cheaters. The train noise drowned out the shots. Clay slumped against the sliding fencing that keeps you safe while changing cars. Leslie opened one side and pushed him out. He fell between the cars and caught himself. He was begging to be pulled up when she took out her knife, grabbed his hair and scalped him. Maybe he did crap in his pants then, as he hung there feeling his life juices running from his body, mixed with terrible pain. Leslie stomped his hand and he fell under the big wheels.

The papers said there wasn't enough left to have an autopsy for the cause of death, but the most unusual thing they found was some how in all that grinding, he had been scalped and the hair had been thrown free. Zeb and the others were being hunted now, but by whom and from where.

Chapter 37

Donna was able to rent Rue 14, right off Bourbon Street, in New Orleans. It was said that it was haunted and no one would stay there very long because the original Cher Pluisant walked the halls. This was just fine with Donna and Leslie since they lived with spirits all the time in their Indian life. Leslie would pass as the original daughter of Miz Cher Pluisant and Donna as Miz Barb Talbott, a ship's captain's wife, whose husband was away for long periods of time. To cover her swarthiness and accent, Donna would be of Dutch decent, from the lowlands of Holland. Zeb Taggert now owned the same bank that the original banker's family had owned.

It wasn't long before Miz Cher made her appearance to the new Cher and Barb. She was startled at how much the old and the new resembled each other when Leslie had on her wig. Leslie didn't have the full lips or the filled out body, but the color was the same. The new one had the stoic stare of an Indian; the old one had the wild desirous feelings of a sex cat. Cher Pluisant told them The Great Eagle had visited her and now he would speak to them through her.

The girls' only contact with family back home was a mailed newspaper they sent once a month, to The Rockin' Jug, or when they got another Taggert, like the train job. That was too easy. They would really have to earn their next victory. No return address, just a paper and their friends and kin knew all was well.

The plan was to get the other two Taggert cousins. They were not guarded as well as old Zeb and also, by getting them first, it would scare Zeb even more. As the Governor, he had bodyguards three deep around him, but they would find a way. The most probable way was through sex or a big money scheme. He was vulnerable to both. The big, greedy, rich would fall for a scam; the easiest sometimes.

The girls were taking New Orleans in. They couldn't believe what they saw sometimes. There were so many diverse cultures all mixed together. You could see families with several kids and they didn't look related after all the mixed genes. As they sat in a sidewalk cafe one morning, there was some big brady men next to them. One of the men were teasing one of the others and called him a damn old cane breaker. Leslie and Donna turned to look at him. Strangely, that is what they called their daddy as a young man. Leslie found herself looking right in the eyes of the biggest, strongest man, of about her own age that she had ever seen. Miss beady-eyed starer was taken aback at his raw handsomeness. The big outstanding thing about him was a big shock of curly hair and real white skin.

She amusingly asked, "What's a cane breaker?"

Big Rafe says, "Ma'am, I guess the best way is to explain it is, he's about half Georgia cracker, about half Cajun, which is part alligator and part bear and lives in the swamp. He cuts timber that gets barged down to New Orleans and gets screwed out of it by a man like Jack Taggert, who controls the lumber business lock, stock and barrel. We been here two weeks, with a barrage of lumber from up on the Pearl River, and they're trying to beat us down to starvation wages. Looks like they may just do it too, as we gotta get back to our families with some supplies soon."

Leslie's blood was stirring. This man attracted her physically, like no other man ever had. Maybe it was that hair. All she had ever saw was straight hair and this just roused her. She'd be getting a line on Jack Taggert at the same time, so she was gonna have this man and she knew just how she was gonna do it.

Chapter 38

Leslie had invited Rafe, the big cane breaker, to Rue 14 for dinner and wine by telling him that they knew a Taggert nephew that was in the lumber business. She said they could help him get a good price for his Cypress lumber and he could help them. She would get Rafe to help them get to Jimmy Taggert and at the same time she was ready for a man. This squaw with Chandler blood had been held at bay too long. This big, curly-haired man would do just fine and then he would be gone back to the swamp and not be in their way.

Donna had joined the Royal Racket Club where Jim Taggert was known to hang out regular. He was also a womanizer and what better place than here to find the youngest and prettiest women in all of New Orleans. Jimmy had seen this dark skinned redhead before and when she came in dressed in a green velvet dress, she nearly took his breath away. Donna ignored him at first but she knew she had him hooked. Women just know these things. She stayed later than usual, as did he.

He walked up to her table after most had left, the gossipy ones anyway and introduced himself. "Evening young lady, I hope I am not offending you. I am Jimmy Taggert."

Donna knew that he was fat and soft after years of debunkery. She introduced herself as Miz Barb Talbott.

He said, "I notice you are alone, are you married?"

She said, "Yes, my husband is a ship's captain and is gone a lot. I get so lonesome and I like to get out a bit."

He said, "I know how you feel. I am married in name only. My wife is physically incapacitated for life and I have a demanding lumber business. Between the two, I must also take a break at times."

He invited himself to her table and with her slight smile; he could tell she was pleased. He had found this ravishing beauty and she was burning up with pent up desire after being neglected for long periods of time. He was sure this pretty hen would be easy to pluck. The right meeting at the right time, but little did he know how this plucking would turn out.

Leslie had Rafe in the parlor, serving him wine. She had made the move to touch him as she poured the wine. Rafe thought, 'Boy howdy!' He was about to make love to a pretty lady of means, and in a place that was like a castle compared to that swamp shanty he was used to. She was gonna help him get a good price for his lumber and he had all ready figured that she had a hold on Jim Taggert. In a little while he would find out how good this Creole really was and get an early estimate on what he might expect for his lumber. Women were lovers; men were users.

Leslie went into the kitchen to check the roast. Meanwhile, Rafe sensed a coolness about where he was sitting in the parlor, even though his passion and wine had him nearly sweating. As Leslie came back in the room, he turned as a cool breeze hit him. She stood across from him, but she seemed changed somehow. She looked like a much wilder and sexier woman than before. Then he realized this was an apparition. Damn almighty, he knew this had been too good to be true. This was a ghost! Rafe bolted for the door and ran as fast as he could run. He heard someone say 'wait,' but that only made him go faster. Leslie had grabbed her gun as the door slammed, when Rafe ran out.

By the time she knew what was happening; he was a block away. She was so mad, she fired over his head and he ran faster, but no one paid any attention. It wasn't unusual to hear fast footsteps and shots being fired in New Orleans after dark. Damn, she knew better than to mix business with pleasure. As she walked back by the parlor, a cool spot was by the door and Cher Pluisant was just leaving. Leslie suspected what may have happened.

The trap was set. The next day, Leslie went to see Rafe. He almost ran off again, but she apologized to him. She should have told him about Cher Pluisant. He wanted to believe her, but kept a few feet between them. These swamp men were raised hearing about and seeing voodoo and were superstitious as hell. She told him that she could still get him a decent price. He was to call on Jim Taggert late that evening, tell him that he had to leave that night and that he was ready to sell at Taggert's price. Jim Taggert told Rafe they would get his money for him and bring it by the steamboat landing and he could be gone.

It was done. Donna sent a note to Jim Taggert telling him that if he wanted her, it had to be soon. Her husband would be docking the next day and would stay for several weeks. Jim sent a note right back that he had a late business appointment and would she come by his office? He didn't want to waste no time.

A quarter after eight that evening, Donna let herself into his office with Leslie behind her. Jim heard her come in. Rafe hadn't showed up yet and this was irritating him. He wanted him out of the way. Jim bound up from behind his desk and embraced Donna for the very first time. He was so ready for her that he was trembling. That's when he discovered Leslie behind her.

He says, "You brought company? Why? Who is this Creole with you?"

Leslie stuck her gun in his belly and pulled her wig off at the same time. She said, "I am Leslie Chandler." He got that same look on his face, like he was crapping his pants.

They told him to sit down. They wanted three times the cash that he had offered Rafe for his lumber. Jim eagerly counted out the cash. This was just robbery and he could get his money back. He knew where they lived and Uncle Zeb had power. They told him to close the safe. They didn't want the other money and they didn't want this to look like a robbery. That's when Jim Taggert got that look on his face again.

Now Jim was the one that had kept their daddy's hand in that jar, pickled in formaldehyde. He used to show it to his friends and laugh. It was setting on a shelf behind his desk, for all to see. Donna got it and took the lid off of it. She poured a big glass full of the liquid and told Jim Taggert to start drinking. He looked miserable, but started drinking it. He tried to throw up, but was handed another glass. By this time, his stomach was nearly paralyzed and he couldn't vomit. Formaldehyde is a deadly poison and the pain was unbearable. He had fallen to the floor and was thrashing about. He started begging them to just kill him.

While he still lived, they scalped him. They had counted coup. He was soon dead. They put a knife in one of his hands and his scalp in the other. They left a voodoo doll on his desk with pins sticking in its throat and hands. They picked up Rafe's money, walked to the docks and gave Rafe his money. They caught a hack back to Rue 14. When they walked down the hall, there was a rustling in the parlor and light laughter.

The papers had a field day with the story. It seemed that Jim Taggert had been under a voodoo spell and had committed suicide by drinking poison formaldehyde from a jar that had held a pickled hand. He had acquired the hand long before under strange circumstances. He had even scalped himself in the process.

Killing the ones that needed it was getting easier. They mailed off a paper to The Rockin' Jug.

Chapter 39

A couple months had hardly passed, when the girls were back drinking that New Orleans coffee at their favorite sidewalk cafe and who shows up, but Rafe. He hadn't forgotten Leslie and the good money he had made. He had driven his fellow cane breakers and they soon had another barge of lumber. They floated it down the Pearl River, into the Mississippi and on to New Orleans. He later heard about the bizarre death of Jim Taggert, but hell, he was a no good and got what he deserved. There was Ron Taggert still left and then the big fist. By this time the two remaining Taggerts were nearly paranoid with fear. This was just what the girls wanted. Zeb was spending a fortune on detectives, but never got a lead. Loosing his money made him even more furious and he had to recoup. He started more kickback scams. Even above the number of scams that were built into the system, that he inherited, when he became Louisiana's governor. You have to be one of them, bought and sold, or you could never get there in the first place.

Ron was a big water fowler; shooting ducks and geese in the marsh was almost a religion to some. There were thousands of ducks and geese of all sorts that migrated to the gulf coast in the winter. There were no limits and shooting became addictive. The rich sportsmen all had duck camps out in the Cheneers, in the marsh. There, they entertained their guests, cooking rich duck gumbos and traded for crabs and shrimp off the shrimp boats. Oysters were just for the taking. It was a sportsman's paradise indeed.

They needed help, so Leslie put the make on Rafe again, but not at her place. It was at Rafe's place this time. Yeah, buddy. This mixing business with pleasure wasn't all bad and the pleasure was even better than suspected. Now Leslie knew why men and women killed for it and as soon as Rafe was himself again, she brought him into their plan. He was to pose as a lumber supplier to Ron Taggert.

Ron had taken over his brother's lumber business after his tragic death. Rafe was to present himself to Ron from up St. Louis way and say he and his wife, Miz Barb Crouch, were die-hard water fowlers too. Ron seized on the chance to ingrain himself with this couple and get Rafe's business. Lumber was in short supply now, as New Orleans was on a building boom. Plus, he had seen Miz Barb and she was a looker. Who knows? It was easy to send off a guest with one guide and then guide the wife on her own to feel her out. A lot of conquests were made this way. These businessmen tended to neglect their wives anyway.

On this day, Ron had taken out Barb and her husband Rafe in his pirogue, a long narrow boat with hardly any free aboard. They were specially designed to not draw much water and was poled through the marsh. To a novice, they were easy to tip over if not handled just right. The marsh grass was just big floating islands with potholes in between. There were big alligator holes in the floating grass and connecting channels that the boats used to navigate the marsh. This day, they were coming back and there were three of them, a big retriever dog, and a load of ducks.

As they passed a big alligator hole with a huge gator poking his snout out of it, Barb was riding in the back next to Ron, who was standing up poling them along. To flirt with Barb, Ron leaned over, touched Barb and pointed to that big gator. Wrong move. Barb gave him a push and he fell headlong into that gator's den. Gators don't usually attack boats, but they do like them retriever dogs and this was a mother guarding her nest. They are attacked anything under these conditions. Ron was gone in an instant and there wasn't anything to be seen but a big bloody swirl. As he was being pushed, it flashed before his eyes that he had seen this woman before. He had that crappy look on his face as he hit the water. The other guide boat saw him fall, but not the push. They had witnesses. The papers wrote up the tragedy, saying this was the third one of the brothers to die a tragic death. They figured that the gator had done the scalping this time and Donna had counted coup when she gave him that push.

The last cousin was the easiest of all. They had made them pay dearly for their mother and father's deaths. Now for old Zeb. This would take some careful planning and they would need the Great Eagle's help. Yeah, buddy. They mailed another paper about the tragedy to The Rockin' Jug in Cheyenne.

PART III

Chapter 40

The girls had been gone a second year from The Rockin' Jug and they had seen some great and terrible things for Indian squaws. They were homesick. They still had the most important Taggert to get, before they felt that their mother and daddy could rest in their graves. Zeb Taggert was getting more bitter every day. He was almost sure that it was the Donley boys or their kin that killed off his nephews. He would never dream it was two young women.

This had kept him from getting a lead on the assassins. He had spent tons of money, but they were damn smart. They had assassinated his nephews tragically and hadn't left a clue. The scalping was the only thing that pointed back to Red Chandler. He had raised a house full of breed girls and Zeb would be next. Damn almighty! Why hadn't he just accepted the fact that his beautiful daughter was a hot-blooded tramp and not started the whole thing. This old 'coon wasn't about to give up and they would make a mistake nobody was that good. He had thought about hiring the last band of renegade Indians in the northwest, to swoop down on The Rockin' Jug and kill every last one of them.

He had spent so much money trying to find the assassins, as he like to call them, that the law wouldn't listen to the crazy Governor any more. They had all been termed an accident, albeit tragic accidents, but some folks just had bad luck. The fire and brimstone Baptist preachers, preached that the Lord was getting his just dues and everybody knew that Zeb was due a lot before he could expect to reach those pearly gates.

The girls talked with Cher Pluisant regularly, it was almost like she was a normal, everyday boarder there herself. Guests still felt her presence and hurried away and that was just how Leslie and Donna liked it.

They asked her regularly, if The Great Eagle had given her his next plan yet. This had to be it. They didn't want to bungle this last job and leave a clue. They wanted it to be over when this was done, but they would count coup first. They wanted him to get that crappy look on his face too, telling them that he knew that he was fixing to die.

Donna returned to the Racquet Club. She was lunching one day and had gotten to be good buddies with the wife of a senator. She confided in Donna that her husband knew all about the kickbacks that the Governor was taking from every contractor and taxing body in the state, but for him to speak out would lead to his quick demise.

Leslie was keeping company with a newspaper reporter. He was writing a book on Creole culture. Leslie had so simulated the disguise that no one could tell the difference. She started telling him about a friend that knew about the scandalous things the Governor was doing.

Now The Governor of Louisiana is all-powerful in the state and can squash most things, but Zeb Taggert had made many bitter enemies. Articles started slipping out in the one opposition newspaper. They knew too much to be totally ignored. They had good facts and a lot of those contractors were talking, albeit very carefully, as you could loose your company and your life. In fact, Zeb had broken some of them by draining off all of their profits, but he needed money, so he gave out patronage to all he could. The rest he just bought and raised taxes on industry that didn't go along with him. He had to have total power. He knew that he had built such a house of cards, that he needed power to keep it that way, or it would collapse overnight. And then, he had those damn assassins lurking close by. He didn't trust anybody anymore. He was making mistakes that he never would have made before his nephews were killed. Accidents, my butt. The haunted house on Rue 14 Street, with the voodoo girls, were brewing up a fitting end for another of the men that needed killing.

Senor Nunez's wife was spilling the beans to her newfound friend. Meanwhile, Leslie's reporter friend was spreading the scandal. They used to pillow talk and he would speculate on the tragic death of those nephews and how he felt there was something there. Leslie knew she was plotting a risky course, but felt that the only way to get Zeb Taggert was to take that risk. Anyway, he hated Zeb Taggert and she had the Indian sign on this boy. He was from one of the most prominent families in town, and he was hooked on her, but would never dishonor his family name. Besides, the girls have come too far to let anybody mess them up now. He was expendable too, if need be. My word.

Chapter 41

Leslie would fast and go in the sweat hoggin', which for her meant, get in the bath tub, cover her head with a blanket, run the hot water through and make steam. A sweatbox was a sweatbox.

Donna would go to the Racket Club. The white half of her could only stand so much of the spirit world and Miz Cher Pluisant's voodoo world, which was on the dark side most time. Oh yes, it could help a love affair or heal the sick; there can be good voodoo. Around New Orleans, you could get most any kind of spell put on someone, for a price. She was ready for some love potion herself; with that Chandler blood was coursing through her veins too.

Leslie and Miz Cher Pluisant, try as they might, couldn't call up The Great Eagle to get his plan. It seemed he was off helping this fellow T.R. get elected President. He held the Indian in high esteem and planned to set aside vast western lands as unspoiled parks and reservations.

The scandals had gotten so bad that Zeb Taggert had been indicted for graft and corruption. He was guilty as hell, but making it stick was something else. The girls didn't want him in prison; he would be hard to reach there. They had brought one of the Big Bertha rifles, fully broken down, in one of their shipping trunks, but they had to count coup. Shooting Zeb long distance would nix that. In any case, he would be hard for the gendarmes to trap and it would be several years in the making. The big old money and their slick lawyers would carry it on till they had him about broke. His teeth would even be pulled to keep him from going to jail. There would come a time when Zeb Taggert wished he was just safely in prison.

Chapter 42

Rafe was back in town with another load of Cypress lumber and he was anxious to see Leslie. Now, the new Miz Cher Pluisant was just about in the same fix as the old Miz Cher and the old Miz Cher was very active. They dare not invite anyone in. This was New Orleans, but too much haunting would draw them too much attention. Hell, it could even get them branded as witches and they damn near already were.

Leslie had to juggle time with the uptown, city boy, reporter and with the big rawboned country boy. The city boy was nice and had been useful for feeding information about Zeb Taggert and causing him more hell. He was also company when Rafe was away a couple months at a time. The reporter was in love, but so was Rafe. What was with these Creoles that men couldn't resist? A lot of them did succumb and married their loves. This is was what made New Orleans the city it was and why it's called *The Big Easy*. Living here was fast and easy, but best be watchful or it could swallow you up and you'd never to be heard from again. Donna was still posing as Barb Talbott and buddying up to Miz Nunez, the senator's wife.

The Great Eagle came back one morning, as they were having coffee out in the back garden. Miz Cher Pluisant usually didn't appear in the garden, but she announced herself with that haunting perfume and coolness. She said the plan was that the Spirits would get Zeb Taggert. That's the plan and it left the girls in bewilderment. So far, she had been right, so no doubt it would come to them when the time came.

Rafe had almost gotten over his fright of seeing the old Miz Cher and wanted to see Leslie so bad; he called at Rue 14. The reporter was just leaving and it was a close call. Leslie could send them both packing, if she so pleased, but she really liked the one and needed the other. Still, Leslie needed to worry about Miz Cher and what she might do.

She was a ghost to be sure, but one that enjoyed a laugh. Rafe wouldn't go in that parlor anymore and he was a big stout woodsman, but he wasn't about to chance another encounter with Miz Cher. He had aged a bunch that night, running for his life, and then having a bullet ricochet off that streetlight to boot. He now sat in the kitchen, but what he didn't know was this house was Miz Pluisant's house and she damn well went where she pleased. While Leslie was in the powder room, Miz Cher came in the kitchen to cause mischief. [You bet.] She didn't want to be so obvious and appear, so she just played the same trick on Rafe that she had the first time, making water in a pot boil with no flame under it and the coolness that tells of her presence and that unforgettable perfume.

Leslie hurried back. Rafe was on his feet and white as a sheet. He was pale skin anyways. He was wiping coffee off his shirt with trembling hands. The perfume smell still lingered and Leslie knew that Miz Cher was having fun and she was furious. She put one hand behind her where Rafe couldn't see and held up her middle finger. A door slammed in Miz Cher's old bedroom. Rafe nearly bolted and would have, if Leslie hadn't had a hold of him. She would get no loving here today, where Rafe was concerned. This bull of a man would fight a bear, but he wasn't coming to this house ever again, not even for the woman he loved.

Chapter 43

Zeb Taggert's world was unraveling. His trial was in full progress and he was out on a million dollars bail, the most ever heard of. He was going to pieces so fast that people were taking bets whether he would last until the end, but the lawyers on both sides weren't about to end it as long as the money lasted. Most of his old servants had gotten scared and left him. He needed a close personal servant and Leslie applied for the job. She would do just fine. This Creole girl surely was safe to have around and she was subservient like the old generation. Yes sir boss, besides she was pretty, young and just good to have close by. He was too shaky and distraught to think of any companionship, but he could set her up for the day when this was over and he had all his power back. He trusted her; his old consort had been a Creole. She had been with him for years, until she had gotten scared and left.

The big day came and the case went to the jury. They were hoping for a quick verdict, since the evidence had been damning to Zeb, but there was one juror that the prosecutors missed. Seems Zeb had saved his father's job and he thought he owed Zeb, so he was stalling. All were betting on conviction at the betting parlors.

Leslie and Donna had packed their trunks and had them loaded on the General Lee, which was bound for St. Louis the next morning, at first light. They had never told anyone where they were really from, not even Rafe. There would be no good-byes. Love struck suitors were dangerous, as they had found out. They would get over it. These squaws would long remember them and this grand New Orleans, but they were Indians and they had already endured more than most, so they could handle it.

The reporter had told Leslie, through his very influential father, that they had got a message from the hold out juror. The verdict would be guilty. The most they could do was give Zeb life in prison, but that wouldn't be too long and Zeb Taggert could snitch to the Fed's. Hell, they all could be convicted as conspirators, as they damn sure were. The Fed's had been trying to convict them for several years, but like most dens of politicians, they were all guilty and wouldn't rat on each other.

The plan was, while transporting Zeb to the stronger jail at the old fort, they would let him try to escape and then kill him to make sure he never talked again. Leslie informed Zeb of their plan. She told Zeb that her friends would cause a diversion and he could get away. She would be waiting with a disguise for him and would take him to her house. Zeb thought, 'My God, he still could pick women pretty good and was it possible he would start over. He could get revenge. It had taken him 20 years once, but he did it and by God he would do it again.' He had the ones burned in his brain that had turned on him and he would never forget. This Taggert wasn't finished yet.

The verdict was read: guilty. The courthouse was a riot of weeping on one side and a gala celebration on the other. Zeb was stunned, even though he had expected it and he slumped like a broken old man. They only assigned two trusted guards to escort Zeb across town to the big jail at the fort. The less guards in on the plot the better. They were to whisper to him to jump out of the hack and run at about the halfway point, but what they didn't see, until too late, was this apparition that appeared in front of the horse's face. It was in the form of a hideous looking voodoo woman. They had just told Zeb to run, but at that moment the horses went crazy. They bolted, jerking the guards down and in that instant, Zeb bolted. Leslie was waiting. She led him to an alley, gave him a top hat and a cape and hurried him to Rue 14. She led him into the parlor and he asked for a drink. Leslie removed her wig.

He was startled and weakly asked, "Who are you?"

She said, "I am Leslie Chandler."

Funny, it had the same affect on him that the three nephews had experienced and he got that crappy look on his face. As they left the room, Miz Cher Pluisant entered it and she had a dagger in her hand. It was the same one that had been used many years ago. She plunged it into Zeb's heart. Now she could leave Rue 14 herself and have some peace. Leslie looked back. Miz Cher had even counted coup.

Leslie and Donna turned and caught a hack for The General Lee. They heard the scream of an eagle high overhead. They found Zeb Taggert a couple days later. There were two men watching the house. One a white man of means and one a big rawboned country boy. The city

city boy finally went to the door and let himself in, hastily came back out and ran away. Rafe could have told him that there were boogers in there, but he didn't know about a dead man. The newspapers had a field day. It was evident to the authorities that there was ghost aplenty in that house and that it would never be lived in again.

The telegraph would stir all the papers. They sent a paper to Squaw Valley from St. Louis and then they caught the train to Denver. They were going home and none too soon, as things were in turmoil at The Rockin' Jug.

Chapter 44

Donna and Leslie really realized they were going home when the train got out on the plains and they felt like they could see forever. They would forever have a bond between them that no one could shake. They would visit Christi in Denver, get them a horse apiece and ride the free range again. They were hungry for their ancestral roots.

What a sight it was, when they first saw the eastern range. They looked up Christi and her husband in Denver and found out that she had two kids and that Jug had passed. Bar had taken over the ranch completely. He was living in Denver and had an office there. He was more into cattle buying and selling than anything else. He said that's where the big bucks were and of course the big risks too. The brothers were only about hands. He had gotten Mandy and Christi to sign over their power-of-attorney, so that gave him six to Leslie and Donna's two. They went to see him and he was set up in a lavish office. He said he was plowing everything back into the company and wasn't declaring any profits to himself or to anyone else, but Leslie and Donna could see that he was living high-on-the-hog, at the company's expense. He was incorporated now.

They told him that this wasn't the way it was supposed to be. That Red and Jug always just wanted a good living and played it close to the vest. They wanted to always have a safe place for the Indian side of the family. Red never wanted them to be dependent on anyone. Bar said, "Well that's in the past. He had power-of-attorney and he was out to make them all rich." Power corrupts sometimes and they never noticed when it happened to Bar. His secretary was beside herself. Bar had evidently told her to look busy and get him after a reasonable length of time.

Leslie got up, closed the big office door and told the secretary not to disturb them until they called her. She got the message from the killing look on that Chandler squaw's face and left. Leslie sat back down in front of Bar, laid her Colt on his desk and told him to undo all the papers. She wanted them back fifty-fifty, like they were when she and Donna left, or he would get a lesson he wouldn't soon forget. He tried to tell them that it was impossible. He knew the crowd he was running with now would laugh at him for giving in to breeds. It would be terrible. He tried to give several excuses, but the two squaws had gone mute. They had spoken, so there was no use in talking any further. Bar was beating a dead horse.

The room was silent for half an hour, with nothing but that constant killing stare of theirs. Bar all of a sudden put together where they had been so long and what they had been doing.

He got that crappy look himself and asked, "May I call my secretary now?"

Leslie gave a faint nod, picked up her Colt and put it away. She had seen that look before and knew she wasn't gonna need a Colt this day. Bar told his secretary to make an appointment with the company lawyers in the morning. They had a lot of documents that needed changing. Damn almighty, what was he thinking? He had just gotten in with the big city boys in Denver and suckered into their game. If he lost The Rockin' Jug, it would be a big loss. Bar would be a dead man now. He had bit the bullet.

Leslie and Donna went to the livery, picked up a couple horses that belonged to the ranch, and headed on the last leg home. They slept under the stars. They roasted game over an open fire and they were in their element. They would forget New Orleans as soon as possible, but one thing they knew. No one would ever lord it over them again. If you tried, you could get that crappy look on your face. Yeah, buddy.

Chapter 45

Leslie and Donna rode up over the rim of Squaw Valley. It was as beautiful as ever, or more so. They would leave it again, but never for long. They were expected. The spirit world had told Miz Donley of their coming. Doc and Frank Donley, along with Mandy and her husband David, were riding hell bent up the valley to see them. They all wanted to know everything at once. Had they heard about the deal with Bar? Leslie told them all that things were back like they had been. Doc and Frank were to go in to Cheyenne tomorrow and get supplies. The old days were back and The Rockin' Jug was back to stay.

They went to see Jug's wife next. She had stayed in her room and didn't want any of the others around. She just wanted to hold them close for a while. Tomorrow they would have a fiesta. While Mandy and the others cooked the big barbecue, Leslie and Donna rode up to Crazy Lake. They visited their parent's and Uncle Jug's graves. They held a scalp dance where the old tepee lodge poles were still standing. They vowed to build a new tepee and have a place to come, to be close to the ones that had sacrificed so much for them, at another graveyard many moons ago.

They made plans to go to the Sun Dance, again in the Black Hills, at Bear Mountain. They had a lot of unwinding to do, but getting the ranch back to normal was the first order of business. Bar had just bought all kinds of cattle. They were gonna build the crossbreeds on Shorthorn and Texas Longhorn back again. True, they didn't bring as much as the purebreds did, but they were a helluva lot easier to raise. They could also make it through the bitter winters that swooped down about ever six years and devastated the other ranchers. Donna and Leslie got a letter by stage, that Bar had closed the office. All monies were in the Cheyenne bank again. They would get new documents soon that would mimic the deeds of old. Bar was glad they woke him up and he was going to college there in Denver to be a lawyer. [My Word]

Leslie had heard that an Indian agent at a near by reservation was cheating the tribe and nearly starving them to death. She told Donna that their brothers could use their help. They would change the look on his face from that of greed, to that of wanting to crap. It was the thing to do for them that needed it. Well, according to Daddy and Uncle Jug, what's the difference if the girls helped out?

Chapter 46

Leslie and the sisters made a new tepee out of steer hides and replaced the old one at Crazy Lake. Leslie would spend hours there, close to Red, Cher and Jug. You could see vast stretches of The Rockin' Jug. It was a thrill to sit and hear the cattle calling their calves, see the weather building up on the far north rim and know that they would soon be getting a shower. The streams would flow full and the high meadows would grow that rich mountain grass. The Rockin' Jug brand was too hard to change, so they didn't have much rustling trouble. The reservation bucks would slip down and pick off a couple at times, but this was tolerated, as they sure as hell needed it.

She would think back to the time when her daddy found her and her mother, after being left for dead beside that Indian burial ground. How a big man had nursed them back to life, she on that mare's milk and Mother on rabbit broth. No one else would or could have stood the embarrassment that he and her mother went through, carrying her like a baby to the potty and then bathing her. How he would just throw a cloth over her face to quiet her down and it got the job done. How he made Leslie a papoose cradle and carried her all most everywhere. She could first remember that broad back, pulling on that dark red hair and how he would just shake his head and chuckle.

The Great Eagle had told her it was time to go help her brothers. The Sun Dance was coming up very soon. Leslie, Donna and Mandylou set out for the tribe that lived on the reservation north of them. An Indian agent, a political hack, was skimming off the tribes supplies and leaving them in dire need. After they became weak from lack of enough food, they became more subservient as history would go on to show, and lose the will to rise up. The government was replacing them under T. R., when they found out what was going on. Leslie and Donna rode into Fort Laramie, went right around the counter and back into the agent's living quarters. They found him sitting down to a sumptuous dinner.

He jumped up and shouted, "Get out of here! I am having my meal!"

"Not any more you aren't," said Donna, as she up set the table in his lap.

The pompous bastard was livid with rage. To think that two sub-humans would dare such a thing and damn squaws at that. He reached for a horsewhip hanging on the wall. He would show them a thing or two. He never reached it. Leslie's Colt barked and he had a hole clean through his whip hand. He sat down with that, 'I just messed my pants', look on his face. These bullies cave in the quickest when they are showed their ways. He was told to appoint a young clerk in his place and then just get out. They would be back after the big Sun Dance and he had better be gone, but first to issue good rations.

They dispatched a letter, with a tribesman, to the stage route and then on to T.R., explaining the agent's sudden resignation. They also explained that they were Red Chandler's daughters, the Red Chandler that he had hunted with. It was nice to have friends in high places. They had to remind each other not to let that power corrupt them, like it had so many through the ages. The Sun Dance that was always held on Bear Mountain was the best in years. The tribes were finally getting better treatment under T.R. Word had leaked out about the sudden re-movable of the hated agent at Fort Laramie and Donna and Leslie were made the same rank as chiefs.

They found some cousins who told stories of their ancestors. They even thought of taking husbands. God knows there were some hand-some bucks that gave them admiring glances. They both knew it wouldn't do. They couldn't be an indian's wife and be subservient to any male, especially as an Indian women were expected to do. The old ways were still followed yet today. These powerful women had seen and done too much. Why, about the time they were married and had a couple papooses, the buck would come home drunk and mean, as their want to do and they would put them in their place and that would be the end of that. A fling maybe but marriage, no way. Hell, they were Chandlers now.

Chapter 47

The Lazy Eight was stealing their grass. The Lazy Eight was owned by a bunch of foreign investors now. They had a foreman that was pressured to run as many cattle as the range would possibly hold. As a result, there was over grazing that hurt the range for several years. They would do this for about five years, make a huge profit and then sell out to a new bunch of investors. These new investors would take another five years to build it up and dump the ranch on someone else. It was a vicious cycle.

The Rockin' Jug saved their high meadows, on their south slopes and turned their cattle in there, to finish fattening before the fall sale. The Jug and Eight ranches were separated by a natural high rim that cattle normally didn't cross. The Eight was running fifteen thousand head, a third too many, even in the best of times. The big outfits tried lording it over the five thousand head outfits like The Jug. They were a cocky bunch. They got in the habit of drifting a few hundred head of cattle at a time, over the rim and on to that good grass of The Jugs.

They would push these small bunches over and hope they mingled in as just strays, until they had at least a thousand head on The Jug. They had started doing this while Leslie and Donna were away and the Donleys were short handed. They would watch for outriders and seeing none, push the cattle over the top. The half starved cattle did what comes naturally. They did this, knowing that come the fall round up, The Jug outfit was honor bound to separate out their brand of fattened cows and turn them over to the sometimes snickering cowboys. What they didn't know was that The Great Eagle was telling Leslie every time they did this. One sneaky way she got back at them was sending about twenty-five of The Eight's cattle over the north rim and onto the Crow reservation. They let the word out that they were sent to them.

Hell they were, but by her and Donna. The Crow were eating a lot better nowadays.

The Lazy Eight had gotten arrogant in the several years, thinking that they had gotten away with this. These squaw men and squaws didn't need all that grass anyway. Now nothing rankles a true cowman like walking on his backside and snickering about it back in Cheyenne in the saloons. Leslie and Donna got out the old long range 45/70 Winchester rifles. There wasn't much cover up on the high rims and they may have to do some long-range sniping.

About four of The Eight's cowboys were holding a couple hundred head just on their side and planned to move them at first light, the next morning. They were bold about it too. No guard or anything and just hobbled their horses. Leslie just wanted to set a new example, that enough was enough. She didn't want to hurt any one of them, if it wasn't necessary, or if none of them didn't need it.

First thing about midnight, Donna slipped in and cut the hobbles on their horses and let the horses go. The worst thing a cowboy can suffer. Cowboys don't walk anywhere and most can't in them boots anyway. They just don't have the legs for it. Next, they got out of their slickers and charged the camp, firing their Colts, but not to hit anyone this time. Then they spooked the cattle back down that mountain. When the cowboys couldn't find their horses, they were shocked, as it was ten miles to get help. They wouldn't be missed for several days at the most, as they were to round up another bunch and push them over, before they returned.

Now a ten-mile hike to a true cowboy is like a one hundred mile hike to a mountain man. They began wondering if they was gonna make it or not. First, they were mad as hell to think that them squaws had the gall to do this. Then they reckoned that hell, they could be dead already. It wouldn't have been no task for them to just shoot them in their bedrolls.

They jumped a deer or two, as they were hungry as hell. They would blaze away with their six shooters, but the average cowboy can't hit the side of a barn and they were fast burning up their cartridges. They finally surprised a jackrabbit and got him. What a let down for hands on the biggest cow outfit in Wyoming. The boss man wasn't gonna like this and there would be crap to fly. If they had only known just whose crap it was gonna be.

Chapter 48

The Eight boys all made it. They had saved three shells and when they finally saw one of there own outriders they fired three rapid shots. That is the call for help in most places and they were found. They were a very sad looking lot. They were almost reduced to crawling. Their feet were a mess. The ones that had removed their boots, to ease the pain, couldn't get them back on. Their only salvation was that one of them was wearing a pair of chaps and they made makeshift moccasins and hobbled on.

The ranch foreman was mad as hell. For one thing, it had happened on their side of the rim, even though every one of them knew what they were doing was wrong. He would show them squaws they'd messed up, humiliating his Lazy Eight hands on their own land. He got ten well-armed men and headed for the north rim.

Leslie and Donna were laying in wait. There was an outcropping about half a mile from the rim, on the side where the Lazy Eights would cross. This was the only cover anywhere around. Now these cattle didn't like climbing this high rim and they had to be hazed pretty good. They would scatter in a minute if they got the chance.

They heard them coming a long way off in that high dry air. Leslie and Donna laid out them 45/70 Big Bertha, long range Winchesters and several boxes of ammo each. Their plan was to shoot enough of them cows to spook the hell out of the rest. Then, if the Lazy Eight men charged, to shoot a couple horses out from under them. If they kept coming, to start picking off the men, starting with the arrogant foremen first. Like Daddy said, we Chandlers don't run from any gunfight.

They had to let them get on their land or it would be murder. The Lazy Eight outfit had bragged on this dirty trick so much that everyone knew what was going on. The code of the West was, if you had been warned not to trespass and you did anyway, you were fair game.

The cattle came pouring over the rim, raising a ruckus and too many to not be intimidating. Damn almighty, they was asking for it and these two hard-bitten squaws were up to the task. The crap was fixing to fly all right. They let them come on, but not too close, just in good range of the 45/70's but too far for the cowboy's Winchesters. Leslie and Donna cut loose. They hated to waste cows this way; this went against all true cattlemen's nature. They figured they would have to kill a few and then the cows would smell that blood and there would be no holding them. Their natural instinct was to return to their home ground, back over that rim.

As the cattle spooked, the foreman spotted where the shots were coming from. He could tell that there were only two gunmen. He rallied his men, but before they were in range, a couple of their horses were killed, dumping the riders. What the hell was going on? Never mind that they were getting in range now and it would be their turn. The first rider that got it was the foreman. That big bullet got him dead center in the chest. He was jerked out of the saddle backwards. He didn't have much time to realize that he was dying. They got another leading rider before the others decided that they didn't have any dog in this fight.

They wheeled their horses around and rode out of range before they stopped. Donna called out for them to come get there dead, that they were through shooting. The girls figured that there was some dirty britches in that crowd. They backed off and the cowboys came and picked them up. Donna and Leslie didn't want them to even be buried on Jug land. They were wrong and knew it. There would be no retaliation; it was the foreigners fight anyways. They had newfound respect for The Rockin' Jug and them damn long range shooting squaws. Damn almighty, what kind of gun were they shooting anyways?

Chapter 49

This fellow T.R. was President now. He had fallen in love with the West, way back when Daddy Red, Jug and them had escorted him on those hunting trips, years ago. He was now declaring new national parks right and left. He remembered the Chandlers and Donleys, you bet. He had also heard of Leslie and Donna's work in helping the tribes, feeding them and protecting them. He was about to create a new big park and wanted them to come to Washington to be part of it.

Donna and Leslie had talked about that. There weren't many new heirs in the family and that someday to let The Rockin' Jug be a national park, especially Crazy Lake. It was so named after Jug and Red trips up there to get drunk and unwind. Christi and Mandylou never got into the rough and tumble carrying on that Donna and Leslie did and that's the way the older sisters had planned it. Christi had even been studying high finance and had straightened out the books. She'd found out they weren't rich, but could live without fear of loosing their beloved ranch. The old Longhorn strain they kept in their cattle wasn't pretty to some, but you couldn't tell the difference with the hide off.

They had prospered in this country where others perished. Mandy was just Mandy, keeping poor old husband Dave, guessing. The girls were apprehensive about going far away again. They were safe here and a lot of things in the past could come back to bite you, but the worrisome thing now was those untrustworthy politicians. Who knows what they might dredge up in the past and claim to get back at T.R? They could be trapped in that spider's den, but when the President sends for you, it's your duty to go.

The girls packed their pretty squaw dresses, if those Easterners wanted to see real Indians; they would be the real McCoys. They packed their Colts also. They had carried them so long that they felt naked without them. They were like Daddy Red and they vowed that they would never rot in a steel cage. There were lots of stories of Indians in a battle that were cornered. They just walked in front of a hail of bullets, rather than be jailed and spend the rest of their lives in prison.

They would get the President's ear and help their people, even if they had to sacrifice themselves. The Great Eagle would spread their legacy to all that came later.

Chapter 50

The day to leave had come and Leslie had asked The Great Eagle to watch over them. He had only given out loud cries and flew northeast. She took this as a sign that they would be safe to make the journey. The White Father lived. The girls were still pretty, but they had some character lines that made mature women very attractive and they could stop a train with their stare when needed.

They were carried by wagon to the stage line, then to Denver by stage. Mister Burleigh, Leslie's old buddy, wasn't driving the stage anymore. He had been wounded in a holdup one day and died of the infection, but he had gotten two of the bandits and brought the stage through with his passengers intact. They caught the train to St. Louis. This brought back bad and good memories. They wondered who was parading around the Racket Club in New Orleans now, if Rafe was still lumbering and how the reporter was doing. They were in for a big surprise.

The difference this time was that they took a riverboat north on the Mississippi, then the Ohio. One thing about T.R., he had assigned a couple assistants to see that they had everything they needed. They were chaperoned to the White House parties and the House of Congress. If they thought New Orleans was astir with people, it didn't hold a candle to Washington D C.

The President gave them a reception right a way. This man was as genuine as they come and he put them right at ease. He asked them about family, the ranch and the hunting. He told them he was saving as much of the most beautiful parts of the West as possible, for all time. That a lot of Americans hadn't seen the breathtaking land that they had seen. He felt it was his duty to save it for future generations. If they could see the great West in that condition, they would be willing to protect it for their children. He asked them their opinion on several things. They were very appreciative that he listened. He even asked Leslie about her horse, Tallboy.

You had to watch that handshake when you left. T.R. was enthusiastic and strong for someone with small hands. The old entrenched politicians hated him and they weren't used to a man that they couldn't manipulate.

The girls were escorted to several gala balls and soirees; it seemed all of Washington was a big party. As they stood in a reception line, a handsome man with a beautiful woman on his arm, stopped in front of them. For a second, these two squaws were taken aback. Here in front of them was Leslie's former boyfriend, the New Orleans reporter that helped them bring down Zeb Taggert. He had gotten famous, came to Washington and was the editor of one of the biggest newspapers in the East. Even though stunned at recognizing them from a distance, his years of training had taught him discretion. This beautiful lady on his arm was his wife. She was a southern belle of the plantation class. She had captured Washington and he had married well. Leslie was smiling broadly for a squaw girl. She wanted to ask him about old Rafe, as she was sure they had checked up on each other, from time to time.

He asked them if he could interview them while they were there. They said yes and to be sure to bring his gracious wife along. He just about lost it for a moment, but that reporter training kept his composure and he said, "By all means." He was to steer them to the Congressmen that could help the tribes and ranchers. They were lobbyists and word was out that they had stock with T.R. and brother, that's enough to get those Congressmen's attention. They had to leave their Colts in their trunks because of security. It seems that these rascals had lied and promised so many different people their vote that they were scared that they would be shot. Damn almighty, it would take one of them new fangled Gatling guns, to wipe out all that needed it up here in this den of thieves.

They were ready to leave Washington, as soon as possible. Things seemed to work out all right, in spite of themselves. They were lonesome for The Rockin' Jug and wanted to go visit Daddy, Cher and Jug at Crazy Lake and tell them about the wonders of the world that they had seen. They had looked at the other great ocean, saw the waves racing to crash against the shore, then fall back as froth and go back where waves go and get in line again.

They had seen Santa Fe and the Oregon Coast. They had seen New Orleans, in the south and Washington D. C. in the north and now they were back on their ancestral hunting and burial grounds. As they sat in their tepee on Crazy Lake, in Squaw Valley, they swore to Cher, Red and Jug that they would stay down in the valley. A cowboy was playing the Cowboy's Lament on a French harp while herding cows.

Oh bury me not on the lone prairie.
Where the coyotes howl
And the wind blows free.
Oh bury me not on the lone prairie.